Rocket Ride

Edited by Gio Lassater

Cover Art by TatteredWolf Studios

ISBN-10: 1537500511
ISBN-13: 978-1537500515

Contents

It Slipped Through My Fingers
By Sita Bethel

Alvar found water in a small asteroid too far out from the charts for anyone else to bother searching. It'd taken the entire day to have his drones excavate the chunks of ice from the frozen rock and store them in his ship—a large, clunky cargo-class vessel held together by rust and habit. The ration credits the Martian Resource Corporation would load onto his account would be enough to feed him for three years. He may even be able to trade some of his ration credits in for a small amount of luxury credits. It'd been over a year since he'd had either a woman or a bottle of scotch, and he could really go for both after so much time trapped in his cramped mining ship—though he'd settle for the scotch.

Thus, Alvar headed home in a better mood than he'd been since Willow left him. She'd complained that he wasn't committed, that they had no connection between them. He blamed his job. Mining for water wasn't the safest career choice, and it sure as hell wasn't a 9-5 desk jockey gig. He always blamed his job when another broad swiveled out of his life— Willow, Jenny, Tamera, Judith, Laura, Cindy, and more before that. He couldn't bother remembering them all. They all approached him, asked him for drinks, dates, or dances, moved themselves into his flat when they decided the relationship was solid, and left just as quick. Fuck 'em. A hand job in the shower was quicker and never asked for flowers.

A jolt shattered Alvar's thoughts as dummy lights flicked across the ship's secondary control panel. An acrid smell filled the cabin, some sort of electrical burn out, but he wasn't sure from which of the ship's two motors because his sensors were shot. Alvar gripped the control panel, trying to will himself to stay awake as the force made his vision fade. . His last thoughts were a curse to Lady Luck, who'd walked out on him like every other pair of tits in his life.

Damn. He really wanted one last taste of scotch before he died.

Alvar wondered if he'd gone to hell. In an interplanetary human society where almost everyone embraced philosophy and science over religion, Alvar had the pleasure of growing up in one of the small surviving sects of Catholicism. All the boozing and dicing must have been as sinful as his mother always warned him, because when Alvar opened his eyes, the pain that stabbed through him felt like damnation. Also, a demon loomed over him.

Large, almond-shaped eyes that gleamed like polished amber studied him. Those eyes didn't have irises, only pupils that formed two slits of black in the center, and two ivory horns rose from the rusty mess of hair that fell around his face. His skin was buttery yellow with a fine mist of orange hairs running down his arms. Everything about the demon was warm – even his smell, a heady mix of cardamom and cloves.

The demon's fingers smoothed across Alvar's brow. A black talon tipped each finger; however, the touch felt gentle, calming. It eased the pain in Alvar's head so much that he almost moaned in relief. Odd behavior, both for him to moan and for the demon to comfort him. Alvar blinked. The thing couldn't be a demon, not the way it petted him.

"It's okay," the maybe-not-demon whispered, his voice lush like a caress down one's neck in a dark room. His words carried a strange accent that Alvar couldn't place. "You're safe."

"My ship…" Alvar managed, though his throat burned with the words. He must be alive after all. Only the living could feel that much pain.

"In the fields. I extinguished the fires. I'm not sure how damaged it is. I've never seen angel wings before."

Alvar frowned, wondering if the other man's accent somehow jumbled the last words he said, or maybe it was a mistranslation. Which brought up a good point—how were they talking without a translator?

"Where am I? What world?"

"Danu."

"Danu?" Alvar tried to rub his temple, but even lifting his hand took too much strength.

The stranger, who obviously wasn't a demon, squeezed Alvar's right hand. "Don't move unless you have to. You're burned and the wounds need time to heal.

"Where the fuck is Danu?" Alvar snapped at the other man, indifferent to his personal injuries. He couldn't get home if he didn't know where he was.

"Here."

"Yeah, that's great." Alvar forced himself to lean up, trying to sit straight and unable to manage it.

The other man supported him and stuffed two thick pillows behind his back so that Alvar could at least lie propped up. "Careful. Remember your wounds."

"I need to get home. Shit, I need to get to my ship. If the auxiliary power fails, then the ice will melt and I'm destitute." He tried to sit again, groaning from the pain, but for all the effort and noise, he couldn't move himself.

The other man looked distressed. "Please, I thought you wouldn't survive. If I fail to heal you..." He looked down. "I couldn't forgive myself."

Alvar settled back down into the pillows behind him. "How come you know coin speak?"

Coin speak was the creole blend of Old Earth languages heavily seasoned with words from the other species that traded with humans. Alvar couldn't remember the last time he held a conversation in Spanish, probably not since his mother died.

"Other angels taught us."

"Angels?"

"Yes. Legends say the angels come with their metal wings and help the people. My great-grandmother told me about how nine angels appeared during the famine and helped with the crops. Before that, three angels came and helped the villages during a plague. Every few generations the angels visit. Most of the time, they stay, but sometimes they go back to the heavens."

Alvar wondered about the ones that went "back to the heavens." If no one else knew about the planet, it didn't bode well for those who left.

"Don't expect any miracles from me."

The other male smiled. "No, you're wounded."

Alvar sighed. "What's your name?"

He made a noise, something between a purr and a chirp that ended in a trill of non-verbal music. He blushed as soon as he made the sound.

"You won't understand. Angels can't speak our language. They don't have the vocal cords for it. I'd be happy with any nickname you gave me."

Alvar studied him. He noticed a tail, like a lion's, orange fur with a tip of red as the hair on his head. Alvar had the strange urge to brush the red hair away from his companion's face to see what his ears looked like, to see if they were also feline. Although most of his features were human except the horns and almost reptilian eyes.

"Fuego."

"Fuego? I'm not familiar with that word."

"Mother's tongue, not coin speak. It means fire."

"I like it." He brushed his fingers back into Alvar's hair. "You're not like the other angels."

"That's for damn sure."

"The stories always say they have pale skin and blue eyes, but you're brown all over." Fuego trilled in his own language, then spoke in coin speak again. "A dark angel."

Alvar fell asleep before he could answer. That's how he spent the next two weeks, in and out of consciousness and on fire. In fevered delirium he rambled in coin speak and Spanish, never sure which was which. Fuego was always there, bathing his face with a cool washcloth, spooning broth into Alvar's mouth, singing in those sweet, trilling sounds that were his own version of language.

Alvar dreamed that he was a boy under his mother's care again, remembering things from a childhood he'd forgotten in his adult life. *Tostones y frijoles;* the Our Father prayer from beginning to end; his best friend, Carlos. As a boy, he and Carlos never left each other's sides. They ran everywhere, hand in hand, until his mother forbade them to play together.

It's a sin, mijo, a sin.

Alvar never understood why being happy was a sin.

He wasn't sure if the tears were from the dream or the fever, but each time they seared his cheeks, cool fingers and alien singing would calm Alvar until he went back to sleep.

Then one day he woke up without a fever. He tried to sit up, and this time managed it. Alvar looked around the room. Tight-stacked stones created the walls and a hearth. A fire burned beneath a large, iron cauldron. He should have guessed by the strange angel nonsense that it was a primitive planet. Alvar's stomach wrenched as his chances of getting home dwindled.

Fuego walked into the room. He grinned when he saw Alvar sitting up. "Your fever broke. I'm relieved."

Alvar looked down, noticing the bandages wrapped around his chest and down his left arm. "Guess I owe you some thanks."

"No." Fuego knelt beside the feather-stuffed mattress keeping Alvar off the stone floor. Fuego set a ceramic bowl and stack of linen strips beside him. "It's been an honor to care for you, dark angel."

"Alvar. My name is Alvar. The angel nonsense needs to stop right now."

"But the legends say—"

"My mother used to tell me stories about demons. They had horns, tails, and claws. Are you a demon?"

Fuego fidgeted with the bandages. "Some might think so. I'm an outcast from the village."

Alvar frowned. "Why?"

Fuego shrugged; he looked miserable. "I refuse to mate with a woman and give her children. Children are the pride and wealth of every village. Anyone who can't or won't provide their village with offspring is exiled."

"Well, shit, I'd be outcast as well. Who wants squalling brats keeping them up at night?"

Fuego grinned at that, but then his face grew bashful. "I need to change your bandages. You were unconscious before."

Alvar clenched his jaw. "Well, I hate feeling like an invalid, but I guess we have no choice."

"I'll be gentle."

"I can take a little pain." Alvar snorted.   Fuego lowered the quilt covering Alvar's body. Alvar noticed he was dressed in only a simple, linen waist wrap. The bandages wound down his chest and covered part of his left thigh. Fuego began with Alvar's arm and worked his way down. The bandages stung as Fuego peeled them away from burnt, sweat-dampened skin, but Alvar refused to show signs of pain, as he lay almost naked in front of another man.

It's a sin, mijo.

It wasn't so bad to have his wounds dressed by Fuego. His touch was gentler than any public service nurse that ever looked at Alvar. The ointment Fuego massaged into Alvar's healing burns felt blissfully cool against his skin, perhaps a little too blissful. When Fuego's hand glided up Alvar's left thigh, his breath hitched.

"I'm sorry." Fuego winced. "I'll be more careful."

"No, it's… it's fine. Whatever," Alvar muttered under his breath.

Alvar thought his fever was creeping back up on him. His face felt hot, his thoughts felt fuzzy, and for some reason he couldn't stop remembering playing tag with Carlos. They didn't call it tag as children; they called it *you're it.* They'd chase each other around the yard. If Carlos caught Alvar, he'd kiss him on the cheek and say *you're it,* and when Alvar caught Carlos, he'd do the same. It was a game the other kids played in a group, boys chasing girls and vice versa, but Carlos and Alvar had more fun when they played alone.

It's a sin, mijo, a sin.

Oremos a Dios.

She'd dragged him to church, pushed him on his knees in front of a statue of *La Madonna,* and forced him to pray until he fell asleep at the altar. Every day, day after day, until his mother asked him if he wanted to play with the other children, and Alvar answered *yes.* He never saw Carlos again, but why was he thinking about this now?

"I just have to re-bandage the burns and then we'll be done."

"Yeah," Alvar whispered, lost in memories.

"Are you alright?" Fuego leaned close.

Alvar noticed that Fuego's eyes blinked sideways, but it didn't bother him.

"Alvar, is something wrong?"

Alvar shook his head no. "I think my fever's back."

"Yes, there's sweat on your brow. I will bandage you as quickly as I can."

The bandages smelt of herbs, yarrow, mint, tea tree. The scent was pleasant, but not as comforting as Fuego's natural musk of cardamom and cloves. Alvar grew hyper-aware of Fuego's nimble fingers, how they soothed over Alvar's healing flesh without the claws ever scratching into his skin.

You're it.

It's a sin, mijo.

You're it.

Alvar wanted to go home. He wanted scotch and women—two women— with huge tits bouncing in his face.

It wasn't true though; never was. He'd always preferred a bottle of scotch to the tits.

I care about you, Alvar. I do, but when we make love, it's like you're not there. It's like you're somewhere far away in your head.

Because he always was in his own head. He never thought about Willow, or any of the others. He thought about his own cock, hard, throbbing, and veined. He thought about the feeling of his own calloused palm as he stroked himself when he was alone, about pre-come welling around the darkening head, about the way male muscles flexed beneath cotton shirts when lifting freight onto a carrier ship.

Was he breathing hard? Was he panting with Fuego's fingers twining around his chest? With the bandages secured, Fuego pressed his palms against Alvar's cheeks.

"Stay with me. Stay with me, Alvar; don't pass out again."

He was in shock, realizing that he'd spent his whole life chasing tits in skirts because his mother preferred him being a womanizing drunk over being a homosexual. He'd forgotten anything that reminded him of who he was, because she'd made a game of *you're it* seem filthy.

"You're shaking." Fuego wrapped them both under the quilt. He pressed his body against Alvar's, but that only made Alvar's shaking worse. "Come on, stay warm."

"I'm okay," he said, but the words hardly pressed out of his mouth. He tried to think of something that would get Fuego out from under the quilt. "I'm thirsty."

"I'll make tea."

Fuego rushed out of the room. Alvar closed his eyes and forced his body to calm down. Damn him, damn Fuego. Alvar didn't understand what about the other male made him remember everything he'd forced himself to forget, but he hated it. He hated feeling pleasant shivers snake down into his belly when Fuego had lain beside him. He needed to go home. He needed his old life, his old routine, and all the scotch he could drink. He didn't need gentle, black-taloned fingers, or gorgeous, polished-amber eyes. He didn't need cloves and cardamom filling his nose, or to see the storm of rusty red locks spilling down Fuego's face.

It's a sin, mijo, a sin.

Fuego returned with a kettle that he set on the hearth. He prepared the tea leaves as the water boiled. He handed Alvar a small, clay tumbler filled with hot, golden liquid.

"This herbal tea will help your fever go down."

"I'm fine," Alvar muttered. "Where's my ship? I need to see if I can fix it as soon as I can walk."

"A mile from here."

"How long until I can walk that far?"

Fuego shrugged. "I'm doing everything I can. I-I'm sorry. A medicine woman would do better. I should take you to the village."

"Stop acting like you're doing a bad job." Alvar set the clay tumbler down and grabbed both of Fuego's hands before he could stop himself. "I would be dead if it wasn't for you."

The truth of his words sounded profound and naked when Alvar spoke them aloud.

"I—I, uh…" Fuego looked down at their hands clasped together and blushed.

Alvar leaned closer, inhaling spice and wood smoke and hating himself for the indulgence. "I think I should go to sleep."

"Yes," Fuego whispered. "You need to rest. I promise as soon as you can walk I'll show you to your metal wings."

Alvar leaned a little closer still. Fuego's body was lithe and slender, the features of his face smooth, sloping lines, but his hands felt rough. The hands of someone who knew hard work. Fuego's bottom lip shuddered, and Alvar *wanted it*. Instead, he pulled away and swallowed his tea in several, quick gulps. The liquid scalded his throat, but it felt good. The pain helped break the haze of his thoughts.

"Goodnight," Fuego said.

Alvar sank into his mattress and pillows.

It took another week before Alvar was on his feet. He walked with slow, stiff steps out of the stone cottage, wincing each time he pushed his healing muscles too hard.

He gasped when he stepped outside. Trees, so many trees, and the air was pungent with scents. He'd only ever breathed air filtered and purified by machines. Alvar stepped out a little farther, and pine needles crunched under his feet. A breeze ruffled his brown hair.

"You're up."

"What's that sound?" Alvar asked.

"What sound?"

"That trickling."

"The stream?"

"Stream?"

"Water? Am I saying the wrong words?" He made a chirping noise, what Alvar could only assume was the term for stream in his native language.

"No, it's the right word. I've just never seen one. Show me."

Fuego looked doubtful. "Should you walk that far? Perhaps around the garden and then tomorrow—"

"Please."

Fuego studied Alvar for a moment. "Well, if you feel strong enough, but you should lean against me to conserve your strength."

Alvar crossed his arms over his chest. "I can walk."

He *couldn't* touch Fuego, not without every instinct in his body screaming to touch Fuego's thick, butter-yellow lips. Alvar didn't trust himself.

Fuego sighed. "If you feel fatigued, please don't hesitate to use me, alright?"

He wished Fuego had chosen a different phrase than *use me*. They picked through pine needles and tree roots until they reached an area where the trees thinned and the rumble of water grew stronger.

When Alvar saw it, he couldn't breathe. He sank to his knees, leaning over and staring at water so pure that he saw each stone resting on the riverbed and each glint of gray scale as fish swam in the current.

"Oh my God. Oh my God."

Fuego knelt beside Alvar and touched his shoulder. "What's wrong?"

"Nothing." Alvar shook his head. "It's just that I've never seen so much water come up from the ground before. It's, it's amazing."

"This is a small stream. If you walk against the current, you'll come to a waterfall feeding a lake. "

"God, God, I can't tell. I can never tell," Alvar said.

"Tell what?"

"Anything. To anyone. If they knew Danu had trees, and clean air, and pure water, the Martian Resource Corporation would— Not all angels are good, Fuego. Some are fucking bastards. Some would take all this and barter it for credits, and they wouldn't give a shit about what happened to your people."

And perhaps the villagers knew this. Perhaps some tricky village elders made sure those who'd ascended 'back into the heavens" never returned home for a reason. But he wasn't in a village. He was nowhere with an exile, and he could make it home if his ship could be salvaged.

But he could never tell anyone where he'd been. Maybe sneak back from time to time to load water into his ship, but he'd never let them do to Danu what they did to Old Earth. He owed Fuego that much.

Or perhaps he didn't like the thought of Fuego dying in a mine underground.

Alvar stood up too fast. The blood rushed out of his head, and he grew dizzy and stumbled. Fuego caught him, stronger than his thin limbs suggested.

"Careful. See? You're overdoing it. Let's go back."

Alvar leaned against Fuego as they walked back to the cottage. Fuego began to purr.

Alvar couldn't help the smile on his face. "Are you purring?"

"Uhh, I, um. I'm sorry. I can't help it. It, it just happens sometimes."

"When you're happy, right?"

Pink washed over Fuego's already fiery complexion. The noise stopped as soon as anxiety overtook his previous calm.

"Don't stop it," Alvar said. "I like it."

"I can't start or stop it. It just happens," he said, pulling Alvar back inside and rushing him to his bed. "Lay down. I'll go fix supper."

The food tasted better on Danu. No dehydrated rations, real vegetables grown in the garden behind the cottage, real fish from the stream, real milk and cheese from the sheep-like creatures Fuego kept in a small barn. Fuego baked bread in the hearth in the evenings and the smell of it made Alvar's mouth water.

Five days later, Fuego showed Alvar the field in which he found Alvar and his crashed ship. Smoke damaged most of the cabin, and the starboard motor—a huge cylinder on the side of the ship in a chrome casing that no amount of imagination could make look like angel wings—had a hole blown in it. Nonetheless, he had the parts and tools to rebuild a motor, and the ice remained frozen.

He was going home. Going home *and* getting paid. He needed a few weeks to fix the ship, but he could go home. The thought filled him with such joy that he grabbed Fuego and lifted him into the air. Fuego cried out when his feet left the ground. Alvar set him down.

"Sorry. I got carried away." Alvar scratched the back of his scalp, looking sheepish.

Fuego blushed and walked away. Alvar could hear him purring.

Alvar spent his days working on the motor, and spent his evenings eating supper with Fuego. They often played card games until the fire burned low and it was time to sleep. Sometimes Alvar brought pieces home to clean and get ready for rebuilding the motor. Fuego would always point to each one and ask what it was, what it would do.

"And those small ones?"

"Those are just bolts. They're easy to find where I come from, but if I lose even one of them here, then I'm fucked. I don't have any spares, and flying my ship with a missing bolt would be suicide."

"They're so small. Aren't you afraid of dropping one?"

"No." Alvar smirked and winked at Fuego. "I'm very sure with my hands."

He had to *stop it*. Stop flirting with Fuego. Alvar was leaving as soon as he made repairs. He was getting the fuck away from Fuego, away from Danu, and away from his own feelings. He was going to fly into a bottle of scotch and never crawl out again. He'd given up on ever being with a woman. He just had no will to maintain the pretense anymore. At this point, he just wanted a stable relationship with alcoholism.

The next day Alvar chopped wood for the hearth. The weather always maintained a chill in the air, and Fuego kept the hearth lit day and night. Alvar felt that he had to do something to help around the cottage. Fuego fed him, and brought water from the stream to heat up for a bath when Alvar came home from greasy mechanic's work. The least he could do was chop the wood for the hearth.

Sweat streamed down Alvar's chest by the time he finished; dirt clung to his chest and arms from the split logs. He'd discarded his shirt twenty minutes into the chore, and he didn't bother putting it back on since he needed to clean up. Alvar stored the ax, smeared sweat off his brow with the back of his arm, and carried two bundles of wood inside to set near the two hearths in the cottage.

He was laying the second bundle down in his room when he saw Fuego. The other male closed his almond eyes and inhaled. "Mmmm, you smell good."

The bold, uncharacteristic statement out of Fuego made Alvar stop in his tracks, confused. "Are you kidding? I smell like dirt and sweat."

Fuego's eyes looked glazed and drunk. He grabbed Alvar's shoulders and nuzzled Alvar's neck. "No, no, you smell incredible. I can't describe it, but… mmmm."

Alvar made a noise in the back of his throat; the sound could have been an argument or acquiescence. He didn't know himself. Fuego continued to nuzzle at Alvar's throat, slowly trailing his nose up to Alvar's jaw. Alvar's mouth parted, and he closed his eyes. He couldn't move. No, he didn't *want* to move. He enjoyed the way Fuego clutched at his shoulders and more so the way Fuego's nose brushed against his cheek.

Fuego purred, loud, thick, and sultry. Alvar leaned into Fuego's touch, and when he felt Fuego's lips against his own, Alvar moaned and kissed back. They stood next to the fireplace exchanging opened mouth kisses until Fuego's purr stopped and he pulled away.

"I'm sorry. I don't know why— Please forgive me!"

He turned to flee from the room, but Alvar grabbed his arm and pulled him back.

"Don't," Alvar said.

"I'm ashamed." Tears washed down Fuego's cream-colored cheeks. "I had no control. You smelt so good. I don't know why I did that."

"It's my fault," Alvar confessed. Seeing Fuego cry bothered him. "I'm probably…putting out pheromones or something."

Fuego looked at the flames in the hearth. "You're not a woman or even one of my people. I shouldn't respond to your pheromones."

"No?"

"N-no." Fuego tried to pull away. "Let go. You still smell good."
It's a sin, mijo, a sin.

He didn't care anymore. He wanted Fuego to grab him again. He wanted the mulled taste of Fuego's mouth back on his tongue.

"Fuego."

The sound of his name caused some of the tension to release as Fuego stopped pulling away. His golden eyes stared at Alvar, frightened and still glazed with lust. "A-Alvar?"

"Fuego, I—"

It's a sin.

His fingers shook, but he lifted his hand up to Fuego's deep, rust-colored hair. "May I?"

Fuego nodded. He also shook.

Alvar brushed the shag of hair away from Fuego's ears. As suspected, Fuego's ears were feline, rounded like a lion's and covered in soft, orange and yellow fuzz. Alvar used the pad of his thumb to trace around the top curve of Fuego's left ear.

Fuego purred again, his eyes closed. "Why, why are you... Oh Alvar!" Fuego moaned, rich and velvety.

Alvar took a step closer, his own eyes half lidded. "You smell like cardamom and cloves—like exotic spices only the rich get a chance to taste. It's been driving me crazy since I had a fever."

"Please, please let me go. If you don't I'll, I'll, I'll..."

"You'll what?" Alvar growled in Fuego's right ear, still caressing the left.

Fuego's eyes fluttered half open, trying to gauge Alvar. His tail flicked behind him as he grabbed Alvar by the waist and pulled their bodies together. Fuego bit at Alvar's neck, and then down to his nipple, pulling with his teeth until the nib of flesh poked out hard from Alvar's chest. Alvar cried out a guttural moan, bucking at Fuego's groin so he could feel Alvar's erection pressing against his trousers.

Fuego took the hint, pulling them to the mattress on the floor and pushing Alvar down. Alvar tore at Fuego's clothes as Fuego ghosted his claws down Alvar's scarred chest. Alvar's fingers wandered over Fuego's back. Soft fur grew around the area of his tail, and Alvar drew his fingers across the silky patch of hair. His touch made Fuego arch up, his tail flicking in the air.

Alvar wondered what his mother would think, if she saw him not only with another male, but also with another species. No doubt she'd try to drag his grown ass back to church to pray.

Oremos a Dios.

But he was praying they wouldn't stop. Alvar might break if they stopped. The tears he locked up as a child in front of *La Madonna's* altar would burst from their subconscious prison, and he'd weep the tale in Fuego's arms. He didn't *want* that. He wanted to forget again, not through suppression of the mind, but through fingers, and teeth, and their bodies rutting against each other.

Fuego growled, biting and sucking Alvar's neck. Alvar bucked against him, allowing his body to act on its own, finally to break the shackles he'd worn since childhood. When Fuego tried ramming his cock straight into Alvar's ass, however, Alvar squirmed back a few centimeters.

"Not like that." Alvar held Fuego's chest to keep him from trying another thrust.

Fuego panted, his eyes wild and frenzied. "But, I thought you wanted to mate."

Shit, he had to say it like that. Why couldn't he just say fuck? Alvar shook his head. "Yeah, but we need lube, or something. I'm not really sure."

Willow and most of his other girlfriends always used lube. He liked it because it meant he could get the act over with without extensive foreplay, which always annoyed him, until now.

"What's lube? Is it part of your mating ritual? Is it like a nest?"

Alvar laughed. He couldn't stop himself. "We need something slick, or you'll *hurt* me when you enter."

"Oh." Fuego gave Alvar an embarrassed look. "I—would almond oil work?"

Would it? How the fuck was Alvar supposed to know? But it wasn't as if he had access to silicon lubricant anywhere on Danu. "Let's try it," he said.

Fuego ran to his larder and returned with a clay vessel. He broke the wax seal and poured the oil over Alvar's asshole. Alvar used his fingers to push the oil inside of himself, trying to get himself as slick as possible. His mouth felt dry; his stomach tied itself into twitching knots.

Fuego set the jar aside and pulled Alvar's hand away from his ass. Fuego entered Alvar all at once and moved hard inside him. True to his name, it was fire. Alvar held his breath, refusing to cry out as the strange feeling consumed him. It felt like his colon wanted to push itself out of his body to escape the burning heat, but every time Fuego reached the peak of his thrust there was a *something* that lit up inside Alvar and made his cock twitch.

He fisted the sheets below him and grunted, trying to relax, but that was impossible with his lower half on fire. He didn't have to bare the searing thrusts for long, because it only took minutes before Fuego threw his head back, and let out a cry, singing out in his native language as he came hot and quick into Alvar's body.

When Fuego pulled out, Alvar moaned. For all the awkwardness and burning of the act, he missed the overwhelming feeling, wanted it to last much, *much* longer, wanted the pressure in his balls to be released. He reached for his erection, smearing the pre-come along his head and using his hand, still slick with almond oil, to glide down his shaft.

Fuego slapped Alvar's hand away with a possessive growl, but before Alvar could protest, Fuego impaled himself on Alvar's cock and began to ride him. Fuego didn't seem bothered by the fact that he didn't use oil beforehand. He bucked and writhed on top of Alvar, trilling the entire time.

Alvar gasped for breath at the new feeling. It didn't have the same charm as being filled, but the heat wrapped around Alvar's cock felt like Divine Grace. Alvar watched Fuego move, admiring his lithe form. Fuego's erection rose thick and hard out of an inch of foreskin covered in a shag of red hair that ran between his legs in an attractive fringe. Alvar realized that Fuego's dick still stood hard and straight, and then he realized that Fuego's race didn't have the human male issue with refractory periods. After another minute, Fuego came a second time, leaving a string of pearls on Alvar's brown belly.

Alvar needed more. He slammed Fuego into the feather mattress and pumped himself into Fuego's beautiful body. "How many?" he asked, his voice harsh with lust.

Fuego sang as Alvar moved, mewling and forgetting every word of coin speak he knew, but Alvar's question brought a few words back. "How many what? Don't stop."

"How many orgasms will you have?"

"I don't know. I've never mated." Fuego sounded perturbed by the question, as if he couldn't be bothered to translate words when he wanted to mewl out his pleasure in his own way.

Alvar pushed faster, relishing the pressure of Fuego squeezing around him. Fuego came a third and fourth time before Alvar had his first orgasm. Alvar's body shuddered as he came so hard that his vision blackened, and he dropped on top of Fuego's chest.

"Holy shit," he whispered.

"Please, a little more," Fuego begged, shifting from underneath Alvar's body weight and switching positions again.

With Alvar still lying on his belly, Fuego entered Alvar a second time, mindful to apply more oil before he inserted. This time, Alvar's body lay relaxed from the best orgasm of his life, and Fuego's cock pumping inside of Alvar didn't burn half as much. Alvar moaned, spent from his climax, but still enjoying the pressure of Fuego's body as it moved.

The scent of cloves hung so thick in the air that Alvar felt drunk off it. It mingled with the smoke from the hearth, and the smell of Alvar's own body, rank with sweat and hormones, but *masculine* and arousing even to Alvar's nose – especially when mixed with Fuego's natural musk. The fifth time Fuego came he cried out louder than before, his nails sinking into Alvar's hips. He fell away, rolling beside Alvar and gasping.

"Five." Fuego's purring almost drowned out his voice.

"One for me, and I'm good."

"That seems…sad, lonely even."

"That's not how I feel at all." He grabbed Fuego's hand. "I've never been less lonely."

Fuego yanked his hand out of Alvar's and turned away. "Stop it."

Alvar frowned. "What's wrong?"

"You're leaving. I don't want to get close to you."

The words felt like a slap. Alvar turned away from Fuego as well, but he asked, "What will you do once I'm gone?"

"Be alone, like before. We…" Fuego's sentence died in his mouth.

"Mate for life?"

"It doesn't matter. I'm an exile. I wasn't going to have a mate ever. This was a beautiful moment. A miracle given to me by my dark angel, but don't hold me. That would hurt too much."

Alvar couldn't swallow. His eyes closed. "Yeah. You're right. We better not get close."

† † †

A light, restless sleep troubled Alvar's mind. Fuego lay asleep beside him instead of the smaller pallet he kept in the kitchen proper near the other hearth. Only then did it dawn on Alvar that Fuego had given up his own room for Alvar's comfort. Fuego snored, but it was soft, almost like his content purrs. Alvar's chest hurt as he lay half-awake in the cooling room. He crawled out of bed and built up the fire. Alvar stared at Fuego a moment, and realized tears dampened his checks in his sleep.

Acting on instinct, Alvar knelt down and kissed the tears off Fuego's cheeks. Fuego gasped, turning his head so that their lips brushed together. Alvar moaned as the taste of cardamom drowned his tongue. Minutes later, he was hard again, and inside Fuego. He thrashed his body into Fuego's like a drowning man desperately

19

reaching for air but unable to break the water's surface. Fuego came three more times before Alvar finished.

They clung to each other as if the dawn would kill them. Fuego wept in Alvar's arms. Neither slept.

As soon as dawn broke through the shutters, Alvar rose, took a bitch-bath out of a basin, and found his clothes before taking off for his ship. He stared at the near re-built motor, hating the ugly, metallic thing. His eyes preferred trees, fields, and the stream. Fuego mentioned a waterfall. What would it be like to take him under the flow of water?

Would he try to find a lover back on Mars? Some slender, red-haired man from North District?

No.

It would never be as good. He wouldn't purr afterward, or scratch Alvar's back with talons, or chirp and mewl as he came over and over again, or have eyes like jewels.

Alvar growled and chucked his wrench as far away from the ship as he could. He kicked the motor, screaming. After half a dozen kicks, Alvar grabbed the handful of bolts sitting in a cup beside the motor, and he scattered them into the tall, pale grasses.

Why did he want to go home? Why did he want machines, and ration credits, and years at a time alone in space searching for water? He had all the water he'd ever need on Danu. He had *everything* he'd ever need on Danu.

Alvar went home.

Fuego stood in front of the table, kneading dough for the evening's bread. He looked startled when he saw Alvar. "What's wrong? It's too early for you to be back."

"Lost a bolt," Alvar muttered, washing his hands from a basin to clean the dust and grease off them.

"What? What happened?"

Alvar shrugged, a little smirk on his face. "It slipped through my fingers."

Fuego wiped his hands clean on a terry cloth. "Let's go back. I'll help you search for it."

He walked towards the door, but Alvar grabbed both shoulders to stop him. "Leave it." He leaned in, traced his nose up the side of Fuego's neck, and inhaled his skin. "You smell really good."

"I don't understand." Fuego blinked his huge, golden eyes. His expression suggested that he did understand, but he was too afraid to hope. "How will you get home if you don't have all the parts for your metal wings?"

"Don't need them. I am home."

Fuego's breath quickened. He trilled his joy, purring as he bit and sucked on Alvar's bottom lip.

Rocket Ride

Jupiter Descending

By Gio Lassater

Alarms and sirens deafen me while I flip switches and press buttons to the cockpit back to normal working order. Flashing lights and warning indicators on my instrument panels all vie for my attention at once.

"Jupiter to NASA. Come in NASA. Do you copy?" My comm line is dead. No static. No chatter or background noise. Nothing.

I know it's pointless. NASA is somewhere, but nowhere near me. A monitor to my left streams data so fast that I can't make out anything, but I know what it's doing. It's trying to figure out why I'm alive and where I am. I've just passed through a black hole seemingly unscathed. The ship is intact, I'm intact, but I don't know what to do next. This wasn't supposed to happen.

The monitor goes black for a few seconds before the words "Location Unknown" flash back at me in unforgiving, unfeeling white pixels. Location Unknown. Okay, time to develop a plan.

I scan for nearby planets, asteroids, ships, or any signs of life. My experimental ship's sensors are the pinnacle of what science has to offer. I hope that it's enough to find me what I need.

In the meantime, I set the computer to run a diagnostic of all systems while I rummage through emergency supplies. I try to keep the thoughts of dying alone in space as far from my mind as possible. They're there, but staying busy helps keep them at bay.

An alarm from the panel draws me back. Sensors have found something. Already? I don't have to consult the readout to know what it is. From one of the windows above my seat, a massive ship the size of a small city on Earth is coming directly at me. Proximity and collision alarms vie for attention.

Pulling on my headset, I attempt to make contact with the alien craft. I wish universal translators were actually a thing because I doubt English is going to get me very far.

I shield my eyes from the bright lights that spring to life across the wide bow of the ship. I attempt contact one more time, but I'm getting nowhere. Finally, I toss the headset aside and start looking for something to use as a weapon in case I need to defend myself.

The ship shudders and lurches, knocking me off my feet. Artificial gravity cuts out. I stop my forward momentum before I hit the deck and pull myself back to the command chair. The lights in the cockpit and on all of the instrument panels flare brilliantly before going dark. Silence suffocates me.

The ship lurches again, and looking outside I see nothing but darkness for a few seconds before it's replaced by a soft green light that surrounds my ship. The unmistakable sound of metal on metal heralds my arrival in the belly of the beast that has consumed me.

A deep, guttural voice fills the cockpit of my ship. I have no idea how I'm hearing it or where it comes from. I have no idea what it's saying.

I float beside my chair in the renewed silence. My ship is dead. Any sounds from outside don't reach my ears. A soft hiss I don't notice until it's gone cuts off, and I realize that I've just lost oxygen.

I take a deep breath and focus myself. There'll be enough air left for me to get to the emergency canisters in the back. I just have to not get to it.

Shoving off from my chair, I float across the short distance to the door that leads to the aft section, which houses the cargo bay. I slap my hand against the panel to open the door before I remember there's no power. That means I have to struggle to manually slide the door out of my way.

On the other side is the tallest lizard I've ever seen. It's a good thing my suit has waste reclamation built in because I almost soil myself out of fright. Huge green-and-brown eyes set near the top and back of its long head move independently to stare at me. The creature smiles—at least, I think it does—and I clearly see two rows, top and bottom, of pointed, jagged teeth.

"Hello." I hold my hands up and smile back. "I'm Colonel James Jupiter…of Earth. Um, take me to your leader."

My chuckle dies when the lizard's three-fingered hand darts out and clamps a dull-grey, metal cuff around my right wrist. I try to pull it off, and a small jolt of electricity causes my arm to twitch.

It—he?—looks at me with one eye while the other one turns in a slow circle toward the cargo bay. It walks away toward the airlock. Another lizard—this one dark black with purple streaks on its arms and head—brushes past me into the cockpit.

"Hey, this is property of—"

I gasp when another jolt travels from my wrist up to my shoulder. My head snaps toward the first lizard. His smile returns, bigger than before. He waits a few seconds, and when I don't budge, he grips a cuff on his own wrist.

When my brain recovers from the intense pain, I realize that I'm lying on the deck. The outer edges of my vision are tinted reddish-black, and I taste copper. An overwhelming urge to vomit settles in my stomach and refuses to move. My captor takes hold of the zipper on my suit and drags it down. I'm fully exposed to him.

His claws brush over my chest and stomach. He appears to be utterly fascinated by my smooth flesh. He calls to another lizard standing behind him. This one kneels down and mimics the claw dragging action. They share a knowing look before the first one grasps my dick. I expect his skin to be rough, due to his scales, but the texture is subtle, soft. I harden in his grip, and that elicits more chatter and more spectators. They take turns stroking me and fondling my balls.

Before anything comes of the attention, my captor holds up his hand, and everyone leaves. I adjust my erection and zip up the suit. He stands up and starts to walk away. My legs wobble when I finally stand up and another wave of nausea washes over me; that bracelet certainly packs a wallop. It's apparent I'm supposed to follow, and I know what happens if I don't. I stumble after him, tripping over the lip of the airlock. He doesn't try to catch me. In fact, he's already halfway down a metal gangplank when I roll head-over-heels behind him.

I hit the floor of a cavernous docking bay that holds thousands of ships. They're all sizes and shapes, from multiple species or planets, I'm sure. However, the only beings I see are lizards—tall, bipedal lizards with skin colored in every imaginable hue, and chameleon-like eyes. None of them look alike. They aren't wearing clothing, and they don't appear to have insignia or markings that would differentiate class, rank, or even sex.

My guide walks past, grabbing me by the arm as he does. Our wrists lock together with a metallic *clink* when our cuffs connect with each other. I walk dutifully beside him, not even thinking about trying to escape. Where would I go, even if he didn't fry my brain before I got more than three steps away?

Since escape is out, I take in my surroundings. The only sounds I hear are my footsteps on the floor. The lizards move like a gentle breeze through short grass. The air is thick, and sweat drips from my brow, running in rivulets down into the collar of my suit where they are quickly absorbed.

We stop in front of a solid door. He uses two of his three fingers to tap in a complex pattern on a pad beside it. The symbols on the buttons could be numbers, letters, or both, but I'm not a linguist, and I don't have time to study them before he walks me through and down the long hallway on the other side.

I move with him to the far end, to a smaller door on the right. He presses his hand to his bracelet, and my arm is mine to control again, separate from his. The portal opens, and he points inside.

I step in. The door closes behind me just as I realize I've been put into a holding cell.

† † †

Time passes, but I have no idea how quickly or slowly. When my stomach begins to complain of lack of food, one of the tubes of liquid nutrients from my ship materializes in the cell. My captors apparently don't intend for me to die. That may or may not be a good thing. I consume the contents of the tube and do the only other thing I can—sit down and wait.

The door to my cell opens silently, and the lizard—at least I'm assuming it's the same one—steps into the room. He beckons me over, and I don't hesitate to comply. I know he has no qualms about frying my brain. Our bracelets connect again, and together we exit the room and retrace our steps to the hangar.

My ship is nowhere to be seen among the myriad vessels we pass. I still only see lizards moving about the area. They don't pay us any attention. Well, with the exception of a few who may have been responsible for getting me hard. Those few stop and watch us as we walk past. Long forked tongues dart over lipless mouths.

An intricate combination gets us past the keypad and door at the far end of the hangar. Beyond, a long hall stretches out, but this one is different from the one leading to my cell. Long, narrow windows line both sides. As we walk, I can see the openness of space on my right and small rooms on my left. The rooms appear to be crew quarters, but they only have beds. All of them are empty until we get to the end of the hallway.

The lizard opens the door, and I get a better look at the alien standing at the foot of the bed. He's almost seven feet tall and has muscles stacked on top of muscles. Burnt-orange hair hangs in thick strands. His skin is dark orange. Two stripes of red run from the base of his neck, down his broad, bare chest, and disappear into the shiny black fabric of his pants. He's barefoot—his wide feet, with eight toe-like appendages on each one wouldn't fit into any shoe I've ever seen.

Sunset-orange eyes take my measure. It's difficult to stay still or continue to look at him while he takes stock of me. The lizard removes his cuff, hands it to the alien, and leaves. The door closes silently, and I'm left alone to whatever fate the universe has for me.

The alien speaks, and I say, "I'm sorry. I can't understand you."

He nods once and pulls a small blue case from his pants pocket. Reaching inside he removes what appears to be a silverfish and holds it out to me. When I don't move, he wiggles it and beckons me to come closer. I move within a few feet of him. Before I can react, he's grabbed me with a hand that completely covers my shoulder. The silverfish begins to wriggle in his grip, and he holds it close to my ear.

The creature makes contact, and I feel it crawl inside my head. A sharp pain lances through my brain, but before I have time to scream, it subsides. I turn and puke on the floor.

"Now do you understand me?"

I wipe my mouth and scrub the back of my hand on my flight suit. "Yeah. That was a hell of a thing."

He chuckles and releases his hold on me. "A necessary 'thing' if we are to conduct business." He sits on the bed and clasps his hands in front of himself. "Remove the suit. I wish to see what's underneath."

"Who are you?"

His eyes dart to the cuff sitting on the table and then back to me. "Very well, since you're obviously not from anywhere near here, I'll appease your curiosity. My name is Koorzo. I am the owner of an asteroid mining conglomerate. The Aamanti, our hosts, supply me with things I want. You know, mining equipment, new technology."

"People."

"Yes," Koorzo says. "I'm here to test out a new species they found. That would be you, in case you were wondering."

"So, a test drive before you commit to actually making a purchase."

"I'm glad to see that we understand each other so well. Now, enough talking. I wish to see what you have to offer me," he says.

I take hold of the suits zipper and slowly drag it down. The front of Koorzo's pants begins to swell as I expose more and more of my flesh. Fully unzipped, I pull the suit from shoulders and push it down to my ankles. Once again, Koorzo scrutinizes me; his gaze roving over my lithe muscles down to my flaccid dick and balls.

"Turn around." I comply and let him get a good look at the backside. "Turn." Again, I do as ordered. "Let's get you out of that suit." He steps forward and bends down to grab the cloth bunched at my ankles. He tears it away with the strength of a Titan, and I have to steady myself with a hand on his back. He flexes his muscles for me. I'm left standing in my boots.

"Magnetic?"

"Yes," I say.

He picks me up, activates the boots, and adheres them to the ceiling. He bends down and drags his tongue over my dick. I reach up—down?—and tweak his nipples roughly. A purr-like rumbling in his chest causes his tongue to vibrate over my stiffening erection. I moan.

"You show great promise." He moves behind me and separates my ass cheeks. His tongue glides over my hole and presses against it. Saliva drips onto my flesh and causes a tingling sensation that becomes warm.

I wrap my hand around my cock and stroke myself. Koorzo pulls my hand away and jerks me off.

A fat finger replaces his tongue. Koorzo presses it inside me, deep inside me. I grunt and gulp air. He fucks me with the digit while stroking my dick. A dollop of my precome lands on his finger, and he sucks it clean. He quickens his pace on both my dick and inside my ass. I try to warn him that I'm close, but before the words form, come is raining on my face. I lick what I can reach and rub the rest into the flesh of my face and chest.

Koorzo pulls his finger out of me and moves to clean off the remnants of my come. "You taste delicious. I've never had the like."

"Well, if you give me a few minutes, I can give you another taste."

"Truly?" His broad mouth opens into a smile that displays his hunger and two rows of sharp teeth. I repress a shudder and try not to imagine a shark biting off my dick.

"Yes. First, though, if you'll get me down, I'll take care of this." I use both hands to squeeze the bulging crotch of his pants. I maintain my grip while he deactivates my magnetic boots and turns me right side up.

I fall back onto the bed, and Koorzo straddles me. He's looking down at me as I run my hands over the steely hardness that is his erection. There's no doubt he's going to want to use it on me. I only hope I can take it. The clasp of his pants proves problematic, but I manage to release it. Koorzo helps me to remove his confining clothing.

"No fucking way." Unfettered, I realize that Koorzo has two dicks, and they're both impressive. Alone on a man each would be a wondrous thing. Together, on the same behemoth, they're a frightening yet intriguing prospect. Side-by-side, a few inches apart, they sit atop one large sac holding what appear to be three balls.

"You're surprised?"

"Yeah. A vast majority of humans—my species—only has one."

Koorzo pulls off his pants and straddles me, and I'm afraid I'll be crushed under his weight. Instead, he grabs one of his cocks in each hand and rubs them over my abs and pecs. "Well, *my* species—the Chal'vaza—have at least two. There are some who have as many as four."

"Why would anyone need four dicks?" I ask in shock.

"For fucking."

"Well, yeah, but other than that?"

"That is irrelevant. This test is still on going. I feel you should now talk less and give me more pleasure." He reaches back and shoves his finger deep inside me again. "We need to open this up so that I can be accommodated."

I open my mouth to protest, but Koorzo takes the opportunity to fill it with the head of one of his orange dicks. Resisting the urge to gag, I drag my tongue along and over the hard flesh. I stroke the cock I'm not sucking and alternate between the two. It's like a threesome but with only one other person. Koorzo moans and adds a second finger to my relenting ass.

With his free hand, Koorzo begins to stroke and tease me back to erection. It takes no effort for him to accomplish that task. He leans forward, and when he sits back, I slide effortlessly inside his tight ass. I bend my knees, plant my feet on the bed, and fuck him with quick thrusts. The muscular globes of his ass massage my refreshed cock.

Koorzo bends down and drags his tongue over my chest. The tingling, warming sensation suffuses my entire body. I feel high, as if I'm floating just above my own body. At first, I think it's that sensation of being stoned that has me believing Koorzo is sucking his own cocks, but slowly I realize that's exactly what he's doing.

"Damn, that's hot." I increase my tempo and fuck Koorzo's ass with abandon. Just as I near the point of no return, he clenches on me and holds me in place.

"It's my turn now, human."

Panic rises in within me, but another swipe of his tongue brings back the feeling of euphoria. He easily picks me up and holds me to his body. The red stripes that run along his chest generate heat that further aids to comfort me. Deep in the cocoon of heat and bliss, I lean back in Koorzo's muscular arms. He cradles me high above the bed while assaulting my ass with his tongue. His saliva works deep within me, and helps to open me even beyond what his fingers had done.

Apparently satisfied—or just eager to possess his prize—Koorzo lowers me onto one of his dicks. He holds me steady, impaled on just the tip, and flexes. I breathe deeply. The warmth travels down to my lower extremities, and I feel myself open to allow him inside. I'm thankful that he doesn't thrust all the way in, but still he gives me hardly any time to adjust. Within seconds, I sit fully impaled on his erection.

Copious amounts of his saliva cover my chest. I wrap my legs as far as I can around his torso, and he slides me up and down. My hands play along his muscled chest. His nipples twist in my fingers. Fuller than I've ever been, I lay back in his arms and allow myself to be used.

Long strands of his hair brush over both of us. Grabbing them in each of my fists, I use it for leverage to pull myself up, and then Koorzo thrusts upward into me. Just when I think we've hit a rhythm that will make both of us come, he stops. I lay in one of his arms. The other disappears from view. His sunset eyes erupt with a fire that sends shivers through me.

I feel the head of his second dick press against my hole, which is filled to the root with hard flesh. Koorzo begins pressing inch after inch of more cock inside me. I gasp and pull his head down. His tongue bathes me, and I relax. Saliva drips from my body onto the bed below. When Koorzo is completely inside me, as far as he can go, I come without warning.

"Yes, human, very nice," he growls.

Come lays in streaks over my stomach and chest. Koorzo licks it clean. Both of his arms support me again, and he continues to fuck me.

Both of his dicks slide in and out of me in unison. A painful sensation quickly turns to pleasure. Every few minutes Koorzo licks me, but the sensation no longer provides the high it once did.

"I am going to come," Koorzo shouts. He pulls me down and holds me close to him. His entire body shakes with orgasm, and all three of his balls unleash a tidal wave of come inside me. It fills me and runs in a torrent from my body and down Koorzo's legs. New warmth spreads through my body. Unconsciousness pulls at the edges of my mind.

Once I return to my senses, I'm lying on the soaked bed. Koorzo, one dick inside me, fucks me slowly. He smiles down at me and massages my chest and stomach.

"You are a good fuck, human. I have already informed the Aamanti of my intention to purchase you." His eyes burst with fire, and another jet of come fills me.

I grab onto his arms and pull myself upward until I sit with him deep inside me. He flexes his cock and smiles when I moan. "I hope you got a good price for me."

He turns so that I can see the window behind him. The hallway is packed with Aamanti. They jostle each other for a better vantage point. Those in front are pressed against the glass to the point I wonder if they can breathe.

"You're the most expensive thing I've ever purchased," Koorzo says.

Rocket Ride

White Knight

By E.V. Grove

I spent most of my time on the observation deck, watching the trails of stars and galaxies and whatever else the universe held zip past like fleeting moments. The view put things into perspective and kept me humble. Maybe that's why I was typically the only one up there. Watching space bend around an interstellar ship had a tendency to make the mind wander. I often wondered about Earth. I worried about those who chose to stay behind; what kind of suffering they must be enduring.

It's unlikely anyone would survive, at least according to the Frei'gh. I remembered when they first arrived. Some proclaimed it a miracle. Others shouted of doomsday and the apocalypse, which was ironic given the fact that World War III had started not even a month prior. Both sides turned to their launch codes first, sending nuclear ICBMs hurtling towards their respective enemies. Most of the missiles were destroyed before they could land, detonating in spectacular eruptions in the upper atmosphere. A few did hit.

The war also enabled world governments to test new and advanced magnetic weaponry on each other. Cities were burned and vaporized from thousands of miles away. Nearly two billion people died in those first couple of days.

The Frei'gh said our world was lost, soon to be plunged into an ice age unlike any other in the planet's history, and it would last for generations. Many countries fought the Frei'gh, believing them to be conquerors. I'm ashamed to say my own country led the charge in that resistance. The "alien threat" took precedence over our efforts to destroy each other.

"Excuse me." The voice snapped me out of my trance, and I turned to see Captain Kil'ran looming above me. I leapt up from the bench and stood as tall as I could, a sign of respect, and smiled warmly.

"I'm sorry, Captain, I didn't hear you come in." I felt my cheeks flush as they always did when standing in the presence of Kil'ran. He stood just shy of seven feet tall and had the physique of an Olympian deity. It always amazed me how human the Frei'gh looked. If it wasn't for their soft indigo skin and pronounced facial bone structure, they could pass as one of us. It also didn't help that he smelled wonderful. I noticed the scent when I had first met him boarding his ship. It was powerful, deep, and fresh, like the onset of a storm. It drew me into his very being. He had shaken my hand, respecting human tradition, and I felt lightning course through my arm. I found it difficult to keep my eyes off his physique. His uniform fit perfectly against his body, accentuating every muscle.

"No apologies. You were back there, weren't you? Home?" His exotic accent stirred butterflies in my stomach and, I'm a little embarrassed to say, something else in me as well. He appeared genuinely concerned, and that helped me in its own way.

"Yes, Captain." I said. "I don't regret my decision. I regret theirs. If more had accepted your offer then perhaps the future would be a little bit brighter, a little more hopeful." Kil'ran stepped closer and placed a large, strong hand on my shoulder. I wanted him to leave it there forever.

"Every life counts. You are responsible for many that were saved that day. Give yourself some credit," he said. "You consider yourself average, someone who would not contribute to the regrowth of your species. I disagree, and I hope you will allow me to prove it to you. Would you be able to distance yourself from the observation deck for a while to have dinner at my table tonight?"

"I…" The question caught me off guard. Why was the captain so interested in me all of a sudden? Why not invite one of the ex-world leaders, or a scientist, or someone, well, someone smarter than me? I searched his eyes for some clue but only found a peaceful stubbornness that would not accept no for an answer. I would never say no.

"I would be honored, Captain Kil'ran." I responded formally and placed my own hand over his. From what I had learned so far, the Frei'gh respected tactile touch as acknowledgement, and when it came to the captain, I was happy to oblige this custom.

"Most pleasing. I will have someone escort you to my chambers in three hours." He squeezed my shoulder then promptly left.

I swooned a little. Could it be possible for a human to be attracted to an alien species? The captain had made it somewhat of a habit to have these small conversations since we left Earth, which I just figured he did with all of the survivors. Each time he came, I felt more drawn to him.

My inner voice chastised me for having such feelings and wove guilt around my brain. *With just a fraction of the population leaving Earth, what good is a gay man going to be towards the rebuilding of humanity?*

Shut up. I told myself. *I could easily be a donor. My little swimmers are just as strong as the next guy's.*

I returned to my favorite bench and gazed out into space. This place could clear my mind like no other. Except now, my stomach wouldn't calm down in anticipation of my dinner with the captain.

I sincerely hoped he and his people didn't resent me, or any of us for that matter. There were significant losses on the Frei'gh side during the conflict. Through a joint effort, Russia and China managed to launch a nuclear warhead past their detection grid. It destroyed one of their main transports, a ship that could easily have held over a million of us, and severely damaged several others. The Frei'gh didn't fight back or retaliate. They were resolute in their purpose for being there, and no one knew why.

I could ask Captain Kil'ran that along with the many other questions that had been piling up over the past few months. I thought about later that night, sitting next to the captain as we ate. The Frei'gh, in their intimate nature, never sat across from each other if they could help it, and who was I to deny their culture? I imagined resting my hand on his firm, toned thigh. I would look deep into his opalescent eyes with unwavering confidence and move my hand towards his undoubtedly impressive manhood.

I reached into my pants and cupped my own growing girth as I thought of the captain moaning in that soft and exotic voice of his. With great effort, I restrained myself. If there was even a remote chance of anything happening tonight, I wanted to save my release for him.

My mind wandered once more to the gentle flow of the stars. It was too depressing to think of Earth and the past, so I thought of our destination and the future. The Frei'gh were taking us to a new home, a planet that resided in what our scientists called "the Goldilocks zone." This lush world orbited a young star in a neighboring system to theirs. This planet was "just right" for habitation and would serve as a new beginning for the human race, although I would rather be with the captain on his world.

† † †

The hours seemed to drag by and when my escort appeared I had to restrain myself from hugging her in gratitude for being so prompt. She was tall, slender and exuded the same powerful presence as Captain Kil'ran. Perhaps all Frei'gh shared that ability. She gestured for me to follow, and I acknowledged by touching her elbow.

She led me down an expanse of pleasantly lit corridors. The passageways were narrow which I came to believe was so that Frei'gh crew could touch as they passed one another. I had made it a point to explore much of this ship during my time aboard, yet there always seemed to be more. It was immense but the soft lighting and gentle blue metals used in its construction had a way of making me feel comfortable in my surroundings. The deck plating had a rhythmic vibration that spread upwards into my body as I walked. It was enchanting and contributed to the gentle nature of the Frei'gh. These transport vessels were designed to carry millions of refugees off world, and it was a tragedy that most were not even filled to a fraction of their capacity.

We passed mostly crew on our journey to the captain's table; however, there were some humans along the way. Almost every one of them had the same look, the look of the unknown. What lay ahead for humanity? Would we be doomed to repeat the same mistakes, or would this be the beginning of a new age for our species, standing strong beside our new Frei'gh friends? I shared in my fellow refugees' sentiment. The future was a scary place to tread, but at that moment I had someone who held priority over all else— Captain Kil'ran.

When I entered his quarters, I was immediately struck by the smell of rain carried on the wind as it rushed through evergreens in early summer. Whatever technology could do that sure beat scented candles. I was impressed by his efforts to make the room comfortable. I was also taken aback by the amount of things from Earth he had procured. The room was furnished with inviting wooden tables, granite countertops, and plush leather sofas that just begged to be sat on. The décor reminded me of an expensive suite I stayed in when I saved up to finally go to Vegas. Large, slate blue iridescent plant life with broad leaves added to the rooms charm and gave a more alien feel.

The russet oak dining table had a feast spread upon its surface. I felt like I was home for Thanksgiving. There were loaves of bread, plates piled high with turkey, sizzling steaks, and exquisite desserts. The captain obviously didn't know how much the average human could eat in one sitting. Two intricate, beautiful long stemmed candles flickered warmly at the center.

The captain appeared from around the corner and dismissed my escort, who I forgot was still there, with a touch to her cheek. He dressed casually for the evening; a silky, soft blue shirt clung loosely to his solid upper body and much to my delight it was ever so slightly see through. His pants were of similar comfortable fashion, though jet-black and regrettably not revealing. I shifted somewhat timidly and felt a rise between my legs.

"It honors me to have you here tonight." He placed his hand on my shoulder and gently guided me towards the table, pulling a chair out.

"If I didn't know better I would think we were on a date." I chuckled nervously and sat down, assessing the food in front of me without having an appetite. I picked up a glass of water, not wanting to seem impolite; he obviously went to a great deal of effort.

"I suppose we are in a sense," he said in a playful tone, and I choked on my water. "I could remind you of today's date if you'd like." He smiled, pulled a chair next to me and placed his strong hand on my leg. I shuddered with pleasure and returned his smile.

We ate and talked, and his hand remained where it was placed. We talked about my past and how I worked in construction building fast food restaurants. I was embarrassed about it, but he dismissed the emotion as unnecessary, stating how builders carried a noble responsibility. We talked about how long ago the Frei'gh inhabited a world within our own solar system. They, too, destroyed their planet but were technologically advanced enough to flee their dying home and seek another. We talked about my family and how they chose to stay behind. They sowed seeds of intense hatred towards our saviors, called them slavers instead. His hand tightened on this subject with a comforting grip, and he would not break eye contact with that gorgeous opalescent stare of his.

"I am sorry for your loss."

"I'll grieve for them when I have the time. It's too soon." I placed my hand on top of his and felt the strength of his fingers. I intertwined mine with his and relished in the warmth of his skin. "Why did you ask me here, Captain?"

"I would ask that you call me Kil'ran. You are not my crew, and admittedly I would like you to be more." To my utter amazement, he sounded nervous. I had never heard the captain express anything below astute confidence.

"You have my undivided attention," I said, as if it were possible to accomplish anything otherwise.

"As you already know, the Frei'gh are an intimate species. We express ourselves through touch and rely heavily on expression." He put his utensil down and caressed my cheek gently with the back of his hand. I closed my eyes and leaned into his touch.

"At a young age, two individual Frei'gh will exhibit a bonding pattern with one another which can span vast distances. This mutual bond eventually brings them together, and they become paired for life. Sadly, this does not happen with every Frei'gh, and those individuals lead a lonely life. I am one such individual. That is, until I was assigned to the rescue efforts of your home world." His fingers traced the outline of my ear lobe, and then moved to my hair.

"The instant my ship entered your system I felt the Couvey'fare; the bonding. I never imagined that it could bridge the gap between species, but we are more alike than we know. I believe this is proof that our two species are related. Perhaps long ago some of the elements of life crossed space from our world to yours." He stopped when I took a hold of his hand and brought his palm up to my lips. I kissed him tenderly there, and then placed his hand between my legs.

"That explains what I've been feeling for a while now." I nearly whispered, caught in my nervous excitement. "The moment I saw you I knew I wanted to be a part of you. Whatever this bonding is, I accept it and wish to explore it fully with you." I leaned in and brushed his lips with my own. Warmth spread through my groin as he accepted my advance, taking my tongue into his mouth.

He lifted me up and out of the chair, carried me into his chambers, and laid me gently upon the bed. With passionate curiosity, Kil'ran began to undress me. As he unbuttoned my shirt, he passed his strong hands gently across my bare chest, always keeping eye contact.

"You are so beautiful," he whispered.

I sat up and pulled the silken shirt off his broad shoulders, leaned in close and deeply breathed in his scent that I had come to love. My lips caressed his flawless, hairless chest, and my tongue danced upon his stiffening nipples. He half moaned, half growled and pulled me into a powerful embrace. Our lips met once more, and I pulled his tongue into my mouth to explore every square centimeter of it. The earthen tones of the room melted away and only Kil'ran was in complete focus.

I slipped my hand beyond his waistline and gripped his rock hard cock. He made that moaning-growling sound again and I savored it. Just the act of bringing pleasure to him was a huge turn on. We explored each other's bodies for what seemed like an eternity and yet at the very same time felt like it could end at any moment. The feeling was foreign and wonderful.

When I took his fully erect cock into my mouth, I could feel his body convulse. He grabbed at my hair, and groaned, pushing himself farther down my throat. I took all of him that I could, resisting the urge to gag. My hands had minds of their own and reached up to stroke every toned muscle on his body. At no point did I want any part of my body to not be touching a part of his.

He pushed me back onto the bed and pulled my legs around his waist.

"Are you ready to experience shovra'ta, the oneness with me?" he purred.

"Yes, Kil'ran." I moaned and tightened my legs around his athletic hips. "I am yours."

His cock was lathered in both pre-cum and my saliva so it was little effort on his part to slide into me. I gasped and arched my back as I took him, however the pain quickly transitioned to intense pleasure. He enjoyed my response and thrust deeper, pressing a strong hand against my chest.

"Yes, Kil'ran, oh yes!" I grunted, and he pulled me off the bed as he continued to thrust into me. He drove his tongue into my mouth and held me steadfast in his Olympian embrace. Both of our bodies shuddered in unison. My vision blurred, as if I was looking through a pearly glass. I could have sworn I saw small indigo sparks jetting from his body to mine.

"Your eyes! We are of the Couvey'fare!" He slowed his thrusts and made them long and sincere. Each push was purposeful and resolute. His hands intertwined with mine, and he pulled them above and behind my head.

I could feel the wood of the headboard as Kil'ran continued to fuck me. To my astonishment, I experienced the life of that oak tree and the valley in Arkansas where it grew. It weathered countless storms and saw the birth of generations of life around it until harvested for this very bed; for this purpose of sharing its life with me as I made contact with its flesh.

I squeezed my lover's hands and experienced him leaving his home world for mine. He gazed back upon his azure planet and wondered if he would ever see it again. He knew the dangers of the mission at hand yet felt that pull towards Earth, towards me.

Kil'ran let out a deep moan as I felt jets of hot cum shoot into me, and I shot an equally massive load. It streaked up and across his sweat-drenched chest hitting him below the chin. He didn't seem to mind, and he collapsed beside me. I shared in his ecstasy and pure emotion. It felt impossible to let go of him. I was his; he was mine.

"Please hold me, Kil'ran." I felt tears rising to the surface as the entirety of past events came rushing through—the loss of my planet, my family, my friends. I would never see those blue coastal skies again or hear the roar of the ocean as it crashed against the cliffs near home. I would never smell the hearty spices as Mom whipped up her special homemade tomato sauce. She would laugh like chimes in the wind when I attempted to sneak a taste on a piece of bread, only to be met with the back end of her wooden spoon. It all hit at once, everything I lost; my defenses destroyed by the love of my captain. Kil'ran sensed that through our newly forged bond and pulled me in close to his chest so I could weep.

He held me all night.

Drops of Jupiter

By Gio Lassater

The others have all heard my story before, with the exception of Burmok. He doesn't look too impressed. "It is impossible to survive a quantum singularity, much less use one to travel from universe to universe," he says.

"That doesn't mean that it didn't happen," I say. "Besides, have you ever seen my species before? Ever heard of a human?"

"That doesn't mean anything." Burmok wipes the back of his scaly brown hand over his lipless mouth. I imagine it has the feeling of sandpaper. "You could be from anywhere. There's surgery. Although, why you would be stupid enough to voluntarily look that ugly is beyond me."

"The truth doesn't take that much imagination. I'm telling you, one minute I was caught in the event horizon of a black hole, and the next I'm waking up to an anthropomorphic lizard zapping me into submission with a metal bracelet. That was, wow, four weeks ago. I think." The hard, rocky ground beneath me bites into my flesh, even through the heavy-duty coverall I'm wearing. "After Koorzo bought

45

me, he brought me here. Of course, it was initially to be his sex toy, not a mineworker. He *really* doesn't like it when you try to escape."

Zaral's laughter echoes off the walls and draws several muttered complaints, but not much more. The other slaves know better than to say anything to the massive Cassavan. Zaral reminds me of a housecat on steroids with a bright green mane that halos his head like ammonia lit on fire. His long, blunt-ended tail swishes back and forth behind him in a mesmerizing dance that makes me smile.

If Zaral knew what I was comparing him to, he would most definitely not be happy. I just can't help it. The whiskers around his slightly distended nose twitch so cutely, and his voice—that is both soft and booming at the same time—sends shivers down my spine. Especially when he whispers his plans for life after escaping from Koorzo's mine.

"None of us expected this," Zaral says. The gusto has gone out of his voice, but I can still hear the slightest bit of determination.

Zaral has been in the mines longer than anyone has—six years—and he is Koorzo's prize. Any time new 'recruits' are brought in, Zaral is paraded in front of them as the example of what to be. The others are encouraged to work like him, to produce the same amount of ore, and to be as obedient as he is.

Only I know the truth. Within Zaral bubbles the desire to be free, to roam the space lanes as he once did. He longs for the day when he can crush Koorzo's neck and toss the lifeless body down the deepest shaft.

However, until that day comes, he bides his time and tells me of his past or listens to me tell tales of a planet called Earth that he will never see. That I may never see again.

"You are sad again, James Jupiter." I'm thankful Zaral, at least, can say my name; not many of the aliens can. He scoots closer to me and runs his blunted claws along the scruff of my month-old beard. He says he likes the feel of it, and I like that he eases the itchiness it causes.

He stares into my eyes, and the phosphorescent green of his eyes captivates me. I swear he has either magical powers or psychic abilities, because when he stares at me like that, as if he's plumbing the depths of every molecule of my body, I want to open myself completely to him.

"I miss my family," I say. "I miss Earth, and I know you miss your previous life too. We're not the only ones. Surely there must be a way to get to Koorzo or to get out of the mine." I say the words so only he can hear me. There's no one sitting close to us, but I don't want to take any chances by speaking in a normal tone.

"I have had a long time to plan this," Zaral says. "Believe me, we are close. If you stay by my side, when the time is right, we will be free of this place. Together."

He leans close and licks my lips from corner to corner. It's how he always initiates, and I've slowly gotten used to it. I'll admit it took some time not to imagine a house cat was licking me, but once I did, the passion that came after...

I smile, and Zaral smiles back. He allows me to kiss him the way I'm most familiar with, and I remember, almost without thinking, not to catch my tongue on his sharp teeth. Two or three times of a bleeding tongue was enough to learn that lesson.

Zaral's hardening cock pushes through the pouch of flesh that keeps it concealed. I reach down, gently tugging upward on it and enjoying the hiss of pleasure in my ear. Zaral nibbles at my lobe and moves down along my neck, kissing and playfully biting my flesh.

An alarm that reminds me of a foghorn echoes throughout the cavern, and I groan at the same time Zaral says a curse word that my brain can't translate, even with the aid of a subcutaneous translator Koorzo's medic inserted in my head. Zaral has tried several times to tell me what it means, but my mind refuses to understand it.

"Get up, you two. It is time for working, not time for fucking." Mardax, Koorzo's premier grunt, stands over us, blatantly groping himself through the fabric of his uniform. "It's a pity I had to interrupt, but if you two ever decide you want to be fucked like you've never been fucked before, let me know. I have more than enough to satisfy you both."

Zaral pushes his finger to my lips before I can say anything. With feline grace and sensuality emanating from every fiber of his being, Zaral crawls across the cage and sits on his knees in front of Mardax. Staring up at the thuggish alien that looks like a cross between Frankenstein's monster and a burned blob of flesh, Zaral runs his tongue across Mardax's uniform pants.

A long, wet streak forms, and I don't know if it's from Zaral's saliva or from Mardax coming. The shudder running through Mardax gives me a good idea, and I can't help smiling at the moan that tears from his throat.

"Get your lazy asses to work," Mardax shouts when someone nearby snickers. He had no idea that an audience had formed, and that's the last thing he wants.

"You two stay put," he orders, and then he's running everyone out of the room with kicks, bellows, and a few lashes of a laser whip. Once everyone is gone, he turns back to us, wiping spit from his lips. There's a fire burning in his eyes and a large wet spot on his pants that makes me wonder if this is when he will finally has his way with us.

"You've teased and tempted me since day one, Zaral." He winds the whip around his hands, and I can hear the latent energy within wanting to burst forth and taste flesh, to taste blood and sinew. "You walk around here, like you own this place, just because Koorzo lets you think you're actually something special. You and that dick of yours, you need to be taught a lesson. If you don't stop your shit, I'm going to be the one to do it." He glances pointedly at me, and it takes everything I have not to look away.

Zaral growls deep in his throat, and I can see his mane twitch in rhythm with his tale. He's obviously weighing his chances of taking Mardax right now. I put my hand lightly on his shoulder, silently urging calm. Zaral stands up, towering over Mardax, who is secure enough in his position not to be intimidated. He's obviously dumber than I thought.

"If you want this," Zaral says, reaching down to grasp his engorged cock, "and if it ensures James's safety, then you can have it." He slaps Mardax's hand before it can even come close to his erection. "Uh-uh. Not here. Not now. There's work to be done, and we both know that Koorzo will kill us if he finds us not doing it.

"After the shift, you take James and me to bottom of shaft 18. It's empty, no surveillance, very private." Zaral licks his lips and rubs his dick along the outline of Mardax's cloth-covered hard-on. "You think you've got enough to satisfy me and James, you prove it. Fuck me. Fuck him. Fill our asses with your come. Make us beg you for more." Zaral growls deeply within his throat.

Mardax looks at me, and I give him a lopsided grin. I move forward and lick the wet spot on his pants. Definitely come.

"Yeah, show me if you fuck better than Zaral," I say. "Prove you're a better man than he is."

Zaral's tail flicks across my ass like a whip, and I moan.

"Tonight, you're both mine." Mardax steps back and points to the door. "Go work up a sweat and think about the long, hard cock that's going to be fucking you."

Zaral and I smile at him and dutifully leave the room. Outside, Zaral wraps his arm across my shoulder and shoves his tail into the pocket of my pants. His quiet laughter shakes his body.

"Are we really going to go through with this?" I ask. "Mardax will probably fuck us and then kill us."

"Not if we kill him first," Zaral says. The gleam in his eyes could illuminate a planet.

† † †

"Zaral, Koorzo wants to see you in his office." The guard had stopped long enough to make his proclamation and then started to walk away.

"It's only fifteen minutes until end of shift," Zaral says.

The guard stops and turns around. He obviously wants to exude menace, but I can tell that the thought of facing Zaral frightens him. "He didn't say anything about waiting. He said he wants to see you in his office. I would advise you to go now." He turns and leaves a little more quickly than I'm sure he intended.

"You have to go," I say. "It wouldn't do to make him angry. Especially when we're so close to…"

Zaral looks pointedly at me for several seconds before nodding his head once. "You're right. I must go, but you should come with me. I fear what Mardax will do to you if he gets you alone."

"So do I," I say. "It's not what I want, but maybe I can keep him occupied long enough for you to get back. Maybe he'll relish a nice, long, hard fuck with me to whet his appetite for a chance at you." I kiss him. "Go. I'll be fine."

Zaral growls in frustration. He looks over his shoulder at the guard who is watching us around the edge of a turn in the mine tunnel. Zaral hisses and laughs when the guard ducks into hiding.

"Be careful," Zaral tells me when he turns back around. "I'll free myself of Koorzo as quickly as I can, and then I'll come for you. Remember to placate Mardax, and tantalize him with thoughts of having us both. Make up something if you have to, but just stay safe."

"I will." I kiss him again. "Go, before you get into trouble."

He swipes his tongue across my lips and walks away without looking back. From the set of his shoulders and the lashing of his tail, I know he's pissed off about being called away. The plan was set. Mardax was our ticket out of here. He still can be. It's just up to me to keep him on the hook long enough for Zaral to reel him in.

And gut him.

† † †

A few seconds after the alarm sounds end of shift, I feel a big, beefy hand on my shoulder. I want to fool myself into believing that it's Zaral, back already, but there's no doubt that it's Mardax.

"Where's the Cassavan?" he asks. There's something about the way he asks the question, and a knowing look in his eye that makes me suddenly sick to my stomach.

"You know where he is. You arranged for Koorzo to call him, didn't you?" Mardax hinted he might do something like this. I should have realized he wouldn't just threaten to hurt me.

"You and me are going to take a little ride in the elevator." He clamps both of his hands onto my shoulders and presses his flat nose to mine. The stench rolling out of his mouth, along with saliva, makes me recoil, but he won't let me go. "I'm going to fuck you, and kill you, and leave your body where Zaral can find it. And then I'm going to kill him for trying to escape."

"Koorzo won't let you get away with that," I say. I cry out when Mardax puts more pressure on my shoulders. My instinct is to try to get away from him, but I have to buy time for Zaral to get back. I swallow the bile forcing its way up from my stomach, take a deep breath that I regret, and look Mardax right in the eyes.

"You do realize that I've just been using Zaral, don't you? I mean, of course you do." I place my hands gently on top of his so that he can tell I'm not trying to break his hold on me. "You're not an idiot, and neither am I. Zaral was a means to an end, and from where I stand and from what I can see, that's ending. You're it, now. You're the one in charge."

Holding my breath, I lean toward him, wrap my arms around his neck, and kiss him as passionately as I can force myself to. His tongue, thick and long, forces its way into my mouth, almost gagging me. I back away and cover up my retreat by running a hand over his already engorged dick. He's huge, and it's going to hurt when he fucks me, but if I do this right, Mardax will be the one to be fucked for good.

"You have such a huge cock." I close my eyes and moan while rubbing my hand along the length of him through the pants. "Zaral was nice, but he just couldn't give me what I want. You and I both know you can."

I turn around and rub my ass on his crotch. Back and forth. Up and down. Mardax crushes me to his body and dry humps me. His saliva falls onto my neck and runs down my chest.

"So, you like men with power and big dicks, huh?" He licks my ear, and I can feel a string of saliva connecting my flesh to his tongue. "Play this right, human, and I might just keep you around long enough to watch me kill Zaral. Treat me right, and I might kill you quickly once I'm finished with you."

"Keep me around long enough, and I'll help put you in charge." I slide my hand into his pants and try to wrap my hand around his impressive girth. "Oh, Mardax, damn. That is one seriously huge cock. I'm surprised you've never killed anyone with it."

"Who says I haven't?" He laughs and flexes in my hand. "And what's this talk of me being in charge?"

"Later. I'll tell you later. We have more important things to do now. Like stretching my ass over this monster, and killing Zaral, of course." I step away and pull my hand out of his pants. "Maybe you can even fuck me while you choke the life out of him. I'm sure that would get you off like nothing ever has."

"I like the way you think. No wonder Zaral kept you around so long. You're not much to look at, but you at least have some intelligence and ambition." He laughs and grabs my neck, pulling me in for another kiss.

Higher in the mine, dinner is called over the comm system. We'll have about an hour before I'm missed. There's no telling how long Zaral will take in Koorzo's office. I'll have to time everything just right or one of the other guards will be sent to find me. If Mardax is caught in the act, there's no telling how he'll play it off. I could be killed regardless of how well I manipulate him.

"We should go," I say, dragging him toward the elevator. "It'll take a while to get to shaft 18, and I don't know how much longer I can wait."

The elevator is waiting for us. We step inside, the doors close, and I program our destination into the control console. When I turn around, Mardax's pants are around his ankles, and his enormous cock is pointing at the ceiling. Low-hanging balls, full and ready to flood my ass, sway slightly side to side when he spreads his legs and leans back against the wall.

"Why don't you make your mouth useful while we travel?" He grips the pulsating slab of meat, and even his hand can't fit around it. "You're going to have to open wide." He laughs.

Reluctantly I kneel in front of him. He slaps first one cheek and then the other, letting me feel the weight. It pulses in front me, and for the first time, I'm truly convinced that his dick *has* killed people before.

"I said, open wide." He places his free hand on top of my head, tilts it back, and then rubs his pre-come oozing cock head on my lips.

I stick my tongue out, savoring the taste of him. It's the only thing sweet about Mardax, and I take what enjoyment I can from that. With each pass over my lips, he exerts more pressure, and I know that if I don't open up voluntarily, he'll shove it into my mouth.

I look up at him just as a glob of split lands on my forehead. He laughs, clearly amused by his attempts to humiliate me. I open my mouth and allow him to start feeding me. The head of his cock isn't even half way into my mouth when he hisses and pulls me off him by my hair.

"Watch your fucking teeth, you little shit, or I'll pull them out and fuck your bloody mouth." He spits on me again.

"Sorry. It's so big. I'm not used to it." I kiss the shaft and run my tongue along the length. "I promise I'll do better. Just be patient with me." I wrap my hands around his cock, tighten my grip, and slowly jerk him off. "Besides, I've got a hole that's guaranteed to not upset you."

He leans forward and tears the fabric of my coverall, exposing my ass. A thick, calloused finger forces its way into my crack, and slowly circles my hole. His finger is bigger than some dicks I've had back there. He slowly presses against me.

"That's tight." He moans. "Too bad there aren't more of your kind around here. If all of you have asses this tight, the sex slave trade would be a booming business." He slaps my ass with one hand on each cheek and rubs the pain in slow circles. "I'll take it slow. That is a treasure that needs to be protected and held onto."

"But you're still going to fuck me, right?" I press back on his hand and kiss his cock. "My ass is yours, but only if you use it."

"No worries there. It'll be used." He guides his dick back to my mouth. Wiping the spit from my face with one of his fingers, he moves it to my ass and begins to work me over.

I move into a position that leaves me bent at the waist, allowing easier access to my ass. I'm able to get the entire head of his cock into my mouth, and Mardax is leaking like a warped O-ring. I moan with him in my mouth, and I hate the fact that he's actually giving me so much pleasure.

He probably has a lot of experience, though. Someone as ugly as he is, with a cock as big is his is, probably has people closing their eyes to get fucked in the hopes that it'll help them out in the long run. They're stupid if they actually believe it.

The elevator lurches and then comes to a stop. Mardax jerks me to my feet, and then pulls his pants up. With is arm behind me, he pushes me out of the elevator and along the hallway that stretches out before us. It's only lit sporadically because the vein of ore down here was exhausted a long time ago.

"There's a guard room about fifty yards in. We'll go there." He puts his hand on my ass and continues loosening me up as we walk.

I can barely concentrate on where I'm going. Fear and dread should be making me more cautious, but there's just something about the way Mardax is touching me that is making me lose control of my thoughts and actions. I can't explain it, but the longer I'm around him, the more I honestly want him to fuck me.

When we make it to the guardroom, Mardax pushes the door open and ushers me through. I stop immediately inside, and he bumps into me, cursing.

"What the fuck did you stop for? Oh." He laughs softly. "Well, Zaral, fancy meeting you here."

Zaral is sprawled out on a pile of tattered blankets in the center of the floor. His cock has extended past his pouch, and his eyes have a glassy look that I've come to recognize as him being incredibly aroused.

"Why aren't you with Koorzo?" Mardax asks.

"Oh, I told him I had a party to get to, and he didn't want me to be late." Zaral strokes his cock and waves it at Mardax. "I'm not late, so why don't we get started."

Mardax pushes me into the room and closes the door behind us. He leads me to the makeshift pallet and forces me onto my knees at the same time he pulls a chair up, sitting down.

"I want to watch you play with the Cassavan for a while." He slides out of his pants completely, throwing them across the room, and tugs on his erection from base to head. Over and over. "Go on, play. I want to see how the two of you love each other. How you fuck. Let him open you up before I fill you up, human."

I crawl toward Zaral, moving my hips as much as I can to really put my ass on display for Mardax. Hovering over Zaral's cock, which he slides along my face and lips, I free my own erection from the coveralls. Pre-come drips into a small pool beneath me, and I'm not sure if it's the thought of Zaral or Mardax's attentions that have me so worked up.

Zaral wraps his fingers into my hair and forces me down onto his shaft. He likes it that I can completely swallow him to the base. As

55

soon as my nose touches his short, grey fur, I feel his tail curl around my leg, slide along the lower edge of my ass, and then it thrusts inside me.

Mardax inhales sharply. "Damn," he whispers. "I had no idea you Cassavans did that." I hear him spit, and then the unmistakable sound of him jerking himself off fills the room. We're obviously giving him a good show.

Zaral holds me in place on his cock, flexing it in my throat. I look up into his eyes; the lust has overtaken him. When he finally releases me, I back all the way off, gasping for air. His tail leisurely glides in and out of my ass, sliding up along the spot inside me that he discovered drives me insane.

"You should fuck him, Zaral," Mardax says.

I look over my shoulder and press back on Zaral's tail. Licking my lips, I moan, putting on as much of a show as I possibly can. Mardax swipes his finger over a clear drop of pre-come and licks it off.

Zaral pulls his tail out, and faster than I've ever seen him move, he's on top of me. His cock easily fills the momentary emptiness, and I feel his balls resting against mine. He thrusts into me rapidly for several seconds before stopping and slowly withdrawing all but the head of his cock. He fills me again, and again he withdraws slowly.

"You should feel this, Mardax," Zaral purrs. "His ass is so tight. You've never felt anything like it in your life." He drags his blunted claws along my back, raising welts.

I cry out, but Zaral wraps his hand over my mouth.

"Shut the fuck up," he hisses. "You think I don't know what you had planned? I know you were going to double cross me, use your sexual abilities to get Mardax put in charge." He fucks me as hard as he can, and I scream into his hand.

"You're too late," Zaral says. He slows the pace but he continues to slam our bodies together. "*I* am going to put Mardax in command. It's me he wants; it's me he's always wanted. You're just some ugly alien I've been using until I get what I wanted."

His assault on my ass continues relentlessly. In spite of everything, I'm jerking my rock-hard cock, and we both come at the same time. Zaral's yowls of pleasure drown out my paw-muffled grunts of release. Once he's filled me with all he can, Zaral pulls out and shoves me away, hissing at me.

I roll onto my side, panting and gasping for air. Zaral is standing with his back to me. His tail twitches, and I can tell he's tugging on his still-hard cock. He's never satisfied with just one time.

"What do you say, Mardax? Give me the deal you were going to take with the pathetic alien," Zaral says. "I'll give myself to you. I'll give you everything you've ever wanted. Everything you will ever want."

Mardax leans forward, wraps his hand around Zaral's cock, and pulls him close. Standing, he presses his body to Zaral's, crushing their erections in between their bodies while he stares right at me. I shake my head slightly. Mardax spits at me.

"You have a deal, Cassavan," Mardax says. "Let's seal it by fucking the human to death. What do you say?"

Zaral looks at me over his shoulder, and his smile turns my blood to ice, instantly killing any sexual desire I might have left.

"With pleasure," Zaral purrs.

I immediately start backing into a corner. There's nowhere to go, and I have no hope of fighting off both of them. They're bigger and more power than I am. I'm fucked...or, at least I'm getting ready to be, again.

"Zaral, please don't do this." I get on my knees and look up at him with the most pathetic, pleading look I can muster. "I love you."

Mardax laughs. "Love has no place here. Come, Zaral, I've waited long enough." He takes a menacing step toward me.

"Wait." Zaral puts his hand on Mardax's shoulder. "I'll keep my end of the bargain, but I want you to prove to me that you'll keep yours."

Rocket Ride

"Do not test me," Mardax says. The warning tone is one I've only heard him use in situations where someone died immediately afterward. "How do you suggest I do that?"

"Let me fuck you before we kill the human," Zaral says.

"I've never been fucked, and I don't intend to start now," Mardax says.

"It's a simple enough thing. I fuck you, and you get my unending loyalty. Such a small exchange." Zaral rubs along the crack of Mardax's ass and squeezes his cock at the same time.

"Fine," Mardax says, "but go easy. I'm not as big a slut as your fuck puppet human. Hurt me, and I'll kill you just because I can."

Without hesitation, Zaral pushes him to his knees. Mardax leans forward, staring intently at me. The desire to kill me is plain to see in his eyes.

"You're next," he says to me. He grunts when Zaral pushes a finger against his inexperienced hole. "Carefully, remember?"

"I remember." Zaral licks along Mardax's spine to his neck. When he reaches Mardax's ear, he gently bites on the misshapen lobe and thrusts himself inside the virgin hole.

The curse words cause my brain to glitch the same way hearing alien names does. Mardax is sweating and grunting, but I can tell he's quickly getting into it. He's enjoying the feel of Zaral's cock as it slides deeper and deeper into uncharted territory.

Once Zaral stops moving forward, he throws his head back and laughs softly. "You're as tight as the human, Mardax. Maybe tighter. I don't know if I can bring myself to finish."

"Get on with it," Mardax commands. "I'm not going to wait all day for you to get off. I intend to kill your former pet and be back at dinner soon."

Zaral gives two quick thrusts, and Mardax bites off his words. His eyes rolls back into his head, and there's no denying the fact that he's enjoying Zaral's cock. Before long, Mardax is pressing against Zaral and all but begging to be fucked.

58

Zaral grasps Mardax's shoulders and fucks him relentlessly with short, fast strokes that cause sweat and curse words to fly across the room. Mardax jerks his own erection, and within minutes, his come explodes from his balls with enough force to splash against my chest and abdomen.

Mardax laughs, but it abruptly turns into a shocked scream. He looks over his shoulder, and I can tell there is terror running through him. But why?

"What did you do to me?" Mardax asks. *"What the fuck did you do to me?!"*

He gasps for breath and then slumps forward onto the floor. There's no denying that he's already dead.

Zaral stands up, and for the first time ever, I see small barbs sticking out around the still-engorged head of his dick. They retract back into the flesh, and Zaral gasps, collapsing onto the floor.

I rush to him, careless of my own safety, and scoop him into my arms. He feels feverish, but that's not too surprising considering he's just come twice.

"Zaral. Zaral, are you okay?" I wipe my hand along the matted, slicked-down fur of his forehead. "What the fuck was that?"

He slowly opens his eyes and pulls me close so he can swipe his tongue along my lips. I kiss him, not caring if his teeth tear at my tongue.

"For all his desire to fuck a Cassavan, Mardax had no idea about our mating practices or physiology." He takes a deep breath and lets me help him to a sitting position. "It's a...defense mechanism, or sorts."

"A killer cock? You've fucked me numerous times!"

Zaral laughs. "It comes in handy from time to time, but I can control it."

"We should get back to the group before Koorzo sends guards after us," I say, attempting to pull him to his feet. We'll address my potential death from dick barbs later.

"Koorzo's waiting for us, and he's not going anywhere until we get ready for him," Zaral says.

"What did you do?"

"I'll show you later." He rubs his hand through the trails of come running off my body. "First, I think you need to get cleaned up. But only after you get a little dirtier."

First Contact

By K. Lawrence

As usual Dr Thomas Pritchard, xeno-botanist, had drawn the short straw. While his fellow astronauts were exploring and making first contact with aliens, he had been left to patrol the small forest near their landing site and document flora.

His breath was loud in the suit as he slumped through the undergrowth. His foul mood prevented him from noticing that some of the bright coloured flowers turned to follow his path or that the trees changed colour, their leaves shimmering pink and blue over their normal dark green. Big blue eyes watched him from a bloom of the same hue and, just below the bloom, branches formed the semblance of a smile.

Tom noticed none of it. Instead, he was lost in daydreams, fuelled by the movies he had watched as a kid. He wanted to be with the others. He wanted to be the one that found alien life, made first contact, and maybe persuade one to come back to Earth. He didn't want to be the guy who documented an alien species of lettuce, no matter how helpful or lucrative that may be.

The pale purple earth was soft and yielding to his steps and his boots left deep imprints. Roots pulled away from his footsteps. Branches lifted away so they wouldn't strike him in the face If he had been listening he may have heard the gentle, whistling sound of the trees singing softly to him.

A noise stopped him in his tracks. It didn't sound like a threat but it was loud, high pitched and vaguely human.

He crouched down and made his way slowly in the direction of the sound. His heartbeat, fuelled by adrenaline and excitement, grew louder in his ears. He heard the cry again, louder this time, closer. He moved towards it, keeping himself close the ground as he tracked down the source.

He could see movement through the thick green leaves. He parted them, trying to make as little noise as possible.

He gasped involuntarily when he saw two tall humanoids standing in the small clearing. They had blue-black skin and their hair was in thick, multi-coloured braids, one red and gold, the other blue and silver. Their hair was filled with shining bits of stone, metal and, possibly, skulls. They were naked and undoubtedly male, their long, thick, cocks clearly visible from where Tom sat.

Tom watched, transfixed, as the slender yet muscular figures writhed together. They each had four arms, and every hand was busy with pulling hedonistic moans from the other. Their melodic cries filled the air.

Tom had to leave. It wasn't right to squat in the bushes and spy on them, no matter how hot they were. He was a man of science but this made him feel like a peeping tom; a botanist had no need to study the mating habits of the local fauna. He let go of the branches and they snapped back, rattling the whole bush and causing the white flowers within to ring like little bells. Tom cursed himself.

The aliens fell silent. Tom waited, crouched in his original position even though his knees screamed in protest. He started to move on when he heard the bushes rustle. Before he could move, a hand darted out, closed around his wrist and dragged him through the branches. A second hand joined it, holding him fast as he was pulled closer. He resisted and the aliens held their empty hands up. They chatted to him, their voices soft and placating. Neither had a weapon but their claws looked fearsome and their teeth could probably rip muscle from bones. Nothing about them said animals on the attack though so he stopped fighting and watched them.

As soon as he relaxed they released him. The humanoids talked amongst themselves, occasionally throwing him a glance with their large, almond-shaped, eyes. The taller of the two stepped towards him and reached for his helmet. Tom protested but, with an ease that surprised him, the alien undid the clasps on his helmet and pulled it off.

Tom whimpered and grasped at the open neck of his space suit. He waited for his skin to peel off, or his eyes to burst, or some other horrible thing that they had told him about in the academy. Instead he got a lung full of surprisingly refreshing air, considering the heat of the day and what looked like a smile from the aliens.

The taller one reached for him again, slowly pulling one of his gloves off. With the lower of his right hands he held Tom's wrist. His upper right hand pressed against Tom's palm, stretching their fingers out together and revealing that his hand was roughly twice the size of Tom's. The alien said something to his blue eyed friend who made a noise that sounded like laughter.

Tom stood in quiet amazement as the aliens carefully undid the fastenings on his suit. His other glove and then his boots were removed and examined carefully before being set aside. They helped him step from the main body of his suit once it had been pulled down around his knees. They talked amongst themselves in a singsong language that seemed to be mostly made of vowels. Occasionally, they glanced at him, little smiles on their faces. Tom felt no threat from them. They seemed curious, amused maybe, but not hostile. Their touch was gentle; they didn't rush or force anything. It was pleasant.

Tom was soon left with nothing but a t-shirt and a pair of boxer shorts. Standing there looking pale and uninteresting he folded his hands over his crotch. The tall alien, who he decided to call Red for lack of a better name, stepped forward and slowly pulled his hands away. Long fingers slid along the hem of his shirt and he sucked in a harsh breath. Red stopped, golden eyes searching his face. Tom didn't know what came over him; maybe it was curiosity, maybe his long repressed sense of adventure. Either way he nodded, hoping that the gesture was known across the universe.

Red smiled and mimicked him. "Aea," he whispered and nodded again.

"Aea," Tom said as he nodded. "Yes?"

Red smiled wider "Yeeeas," he purred and slowly worked Tom's T-shirt up over his head.

The smaller one, Blue, watched them closely. With a tiny gesture from Red, Blue stepped forward and ran his warm, slender, hand, over Tom's chest. Tom sighed softly and let his eyes drift closed.

Once again their chatter washed over him as they gently pawed at his skin and dark hair. Fingers danced over his mouth, gently parting his lips and pulling the bottom one down just a touch. Hands travelled over his flat stomach, dipped down between his thighs, and tickled sensitive skin, too many hands for two people but each one more than capable of making his skin tingle. Tom moaned softly as his cock hardened.

"Aea?" Red purred from somewhere close Tom's navel. He looked down at Red's midnight blue hands on his hips, over the waistband of his underwear. Tom licked his lips and repeated the word for "yes".

The warm air tickled over his newly exposed skin. He felt his cheeks flush as both of his new companions studied his cock and talked amongst themselves. Red stood again and stepped behind him, his claws brushing over Tom's hips and leaving goose bumps in its wake. Blue knelt in front of Tom and slid his finger along Tom's shaft.

Tom couldn't take his eyes off Blue, even when he felt two of Red's hand's grip his waist, and the other two stroking his back and hair. He felt a delicious sense of anticipation as he watched Blue's hand wrap around his thick shaft.

He heard a soft purr from near his ear and then felt Red's tongue tease around it. The hand on his back travelled down over the swell of his ass and squeezed softly.

Tom's arms hung uselessly by his sides as he stood pinned between them. Blue's hand stroked his cock, gently squeezing every so often. Tom thrust forward just a touch, forcing his cock through Blue's grip. Blue smiled up at him and leaned forward, large sapphire eyes never leaving Tom's gaze.

Tom groaned and let his head fall back onto Red's shoulder as Blue's mouth closed around the head of his cock. The aliens tongue probed the slit before Blue's eager mouth took in more of his cock

Tom tangled his fingers into azure and silver braids. He didn't push Blue's head, just gave him a gentle prodding to move and take more of his throbbing cock. Blue obliged happily. When he pulled back, Tom noticed something strange.

Blue had two tongues.

Tom watched the tongues caress either side of his cock, surrounding his shaft in soft, wet heat. They moved independently, stroking along Tom's shaft and occasionally surrounding it in a wet "O" of muscle. Blue's mouth closed around him again, hiding his talented tongues from view but Tom could still feel their caresses. Tom moaned again and tightened his grip in Blue's hair.

Red's mouth pressed to his neck again and again and his warm breath. Two of Red's hands massaged Tom's ass cheeks. The two on his hips slid up onto his chest and Tom hissed when Red tweaked his nipples. Red's cock rubbed against his ass. Red moaned and rolled his hips causing his cock to slide against Tom's hole.

Red kissed his way down Tom's back and then parted his cheeks. Tom tensed slightly as he felt Red's breath on his lower back. With a quick word from Red, Blue let Toms cock slip from his mouth and held Tom's gaze as he licked and sucked his fingers before reaching back behind himself.

Rocket Ride

Tom sank to his knees and bent over, eager to get a taste of Blue's cock. His fingers closed around his shaft first, stroking the silky skin before he lowered his head. Blue whined and bucked up into Tom's waiting mouth. Tom moved with Blue as he lay down. Blue's legs spread wide as the alien slid his fingers inside himself again. Tom watched the alien for a few seconds, biting his lip as Blue rolled his hips and fucked himself with his fingers. He stroked Blue's cock, dragging the foreskin and exposing the slick, flared, head. He flicked his tongue over it, licking a small bead of pre-come from the slit. He savoured the taste before closing his lips around the head.

Blue whined and pushed up, his thick length filling Tom's mouth. Tom relaxed his throat and let Blue take over.

Red spread Tom open and one of his soft tongues flicked over Tom's asshole. Tom purred around Blue's cock and his own erection throbbed as Red's tongues returned again and again, lapping around his asshole and pushing in against the muscles. He tried his best to concentrate on Blue but Red made it almost impossible.

A soft pressure on his shoulder moved Tom back, he let Blue's cock slide from his mouth. Tom sat up. Blue slipped something into Tom's hand and rolled over, raising his ass high in the air. Tom looked at the little tub in his hand and then at the tight ass in front of him. It didn't take a genius to work out what was being asked of him.

The gel was cool to the touch as he spread it over his cock but it quickly warmed. He met Blue's eyes as the alien looked over his shoulder. Blue nodded and licked his lips. He dropped his chest closer to the ground and wiggled his ass.

Tom dropped the tub to the soft earth, grabbed Blue's hip in one hand and guided his cock inside him with the other. Blue keened loudly and pushed back. Blue was tight; his inner muscles grasped and released around Tom's throbbing dick. Tom pushed in deeper and deeper. He gripped Blue's hips so firmly that he feared he would leave bruises.

He didn't stop his slow slide in until his hips sat flush against Blue's

66

ass. Blue whimpered and rolled his hips, grinding back against Tom with the tiniest of movements. Tom groaned as he drew himself out a little more before slamming back in. Blue released a high pitched whine and latched onto Tom's hands.

Tom's knees scraped against the soft, light purple earth when he spread his legs wider to give himself a better, more stable base to fuck Blue. He found his rhythm quickly and Blue matched him thrust for thrust, keening with every outward breath.

A slick finger dipped inside Tom and he fumbled in his rhythm. Red slipped an arm around Tom's waist, holding him still. He spoke to Blue who nodded and thrust back, hard. At the same time Red slipped his finger deeper into Tom's ass.

Tom gave himself over to the pleasure of his alien lovers. Red's fingers probed deep inside the human, pressing gently against his prostate. Blue fucked himself onto Tom's hard cock. He looked back over his shoulder, blue eyes wide, his mouth slack as he whined and whispered unintelligible words. Tom tried his best to please them both with what little movement he had. He let his head drop back onto Red's shoulder.

He felt Red's fingers slide from him and then the press of his cock against his ass hole. He bit his lip to suppress a whine as the flared head slid inside him. Red made a purring sound and nipped softly at his ear.

Blue and Red's musical words accentuated Tom's sounds of pleasure. Tom didn't have a clue what they were saying and he knew they didn't understand him either. That didn't stop him telling them how good they felt, how huge Red felt inside him, how tight Blue felt around his cock.

Tom cried out as Red's large cock bumped over his prostate. Red made a noise almost like a laugh and drove himself in deep again, sliding over the ball of nerve. Tom's balls drew up against his body. His thigh muscles contracted and released as heat flooded his belly. He rocked between them, his fingers digging deep into Blue's hips. He was desperate to stroke Blue's cock but Red held him fast. He heard Blue whine loudly as he closed one slender hand around his own cock, stroking fast as he slammed his ass back against Tom. His inner muscles tightened around Tom's aching erection and his body went rigid. With a loud stream of musical words Blue came hard, his come splattering over his hand and staining the pale purple ground.

Tom shuddered and spilled deep inside Blue, his voice stolen from him for a second as the shock rippled through him. Red nipped harder at Tom's ear. His cock swelled inside Tom and unleashed a torrent of warm come. Tom whined into Reds mouth as the alien kissed him-his tongues brushing along the roof of his mouth.

When they parted they were both breathless. Tom bent forward over Blue's back and tilted the smaller alien's face to his. Blue's kiss was gentler, his movements slower, but just as passionate.

† † †

The sun was close to setting as Tom manoeuvred his sluggish body back into his space suit. He felt sticky and tired but he couldn't keep the smile off his face. Blue and Red lay together in the sun. The space Tom had vacated between them had been quickly closed. Not that Tom minded; his part in this was done.

He had no idea how to say goodbye to the aliens, who curled around each other, nuzzling and talking softly to each other. They looked briefly Tom, so he simply waved. He wished he could say more, maybe thank them for giving him exactly what he needed after months cooped up in a ship with no one he was sexually interested in, most of whom were boring company anyway. He simply didn't have the words.

Red sat up a little and beckoned him over. As Tom approached Red began to scratch in the soft earth, sketching out little images. Tom studied them, seeing a likeness of him leaving, then a picture of the three moons of the planet, then an image of the clearing they were in,. The next picture was the three of them under the sun, which high in the sky. Red pointed at Tom and then himself and Blue.

"Yeeasshh?" Red asked, his tongues working hard to form the unfamiliar word.

Tom looked at them both, their deep blue, almost black skin, iridescent eyes and slim yet muscular bodies. They were gorgeous, no doubt about that, and if a repeat performance was even a fraction of what had passed between them today how could he say no?

Blue gave him a sleepy smile and pointed to Red's drawings. "Yeas?"

Tom smiled. "Aea," he whispered with a nod. The aliens copied his nod and smiled warmly at him. Tom stepped forward, kissing them both deeply before walking away.

He managed to get deep into the undergrowth before chancing a look back but he couldn't see them at all. He sighed and continued his trek back to the ship.

Tomorrow, he only had to wait until tomorrow If they didn't show and it was simply a one-time experience? Tom decided he could be happy with that. No matter what stories his fellow astronauts came back with he was sure nothing they could say would ever top what had happened to him today.

Rocket Ride

Close Encounters of the Cowboy Kind
By Gio Lassater

Tonight, Budweiser would help Marshall profess his love for Clint. He slammed an empty bottle onto the bar harder than he intended to and held up two fingers to the bartender. She frowned but set the requested order in front of him.

"You ain't driving tonight, are you?" she asked.

"Clint's in the bathroom," Marshall said. He belched loudly and popped the top from another Bud. "Don't worry, Lucy. I may be dumb, but I'm not stupid."

Lucy leaned over the bar and crooked her finger to draw him closer. "You're not going to tell Clint you love him, are you?"

"Damn it," he muttered.

"I thought so." She cupped his bearded cheek in the palm of her hand. The recent coolness of the beers suffused into his flesh, and he realized he was hot. "You can't do this, Marshall. Nothing good will come of it."

71

"I can't help it." He downed most of the beer, stopping only when Lucy pushed down on the end of the bottle. "I have a burning in my…chest when I look at him. Other places burn too."

"They have pills for that."

"Ha-fucking-ha." He set down the bottle and leaned back on the stool. His head dipped backward, and when he felt a sensation of falling, he grabbed onto the smooth aged wooden bar and held himself in place.

"Let me drive you home," Lucy said.

Marshall looked past his nose at her for a few seconds before sitting upright on the stool. "I won't do it. I promise."

"I just don't want to see you get hurt."

He scoffed. "Clint wouldn't do that. He's my friend."

"A friend who's never had a guy profess undying love for him. Let alone a *drunk* friend." Lucy wiped the bar with an off-white rag and removed the unopened beer. "Here he comes. Just be cool, and remember that you're not going to be stupid."

"Not stupid. Just miserable," he mumbled.

Marshall turned and watched his friend wend his way through the other patrons. His gaze focused on the painted-on Wranglers, which hugged Clint's firm bubble butt and accentuated his denim-wrapped package. Clint's V-shaped torso filled out in a broad chest and muscular shoulders. Biceps stretched the fabric of a Tony Lama snap-button shirt. Clint's well-trimmed brown beard hugged a square jawline.

And those chocolate brown eyes… Marshall moaned and adjusted the quickly hardening bulge in his own Levi's. Lucy smacked him on the arm, and he stifled a surprised shout. She wagged her finger at him and walked away to help a patron sitting at the other end of the bar.

"You ready yet?" Clint asked. He sat on the stool beside Marshall. His powerful grip on Marshall's shoulder made it more difficult for Marshall to concentrate.

"Let me finish this one." He sipped gingerly from the half-full beer.

"I'm gonna go pull the truck around. You finish that a little faster, princess." Clint clapped him on the back on his way to the front door.

Marshall forced his gaze to stay on the mirror dead ahead. Lucy was right, and he knew it. He couldn't tell Clint, and there was no reason to watch the hot cowboy walk out. That would just mean Marshall had to hold his own cowboy hat over his crotch while stumbling outside.

He finished the beer in one gulp and mouthed *I promise* to Lucy. His feet hit the floor and tried to go two different ways. A few seconds of deep concentration while staring at his red Justin Ropers helped Marshall stay standing. Two unsteady steps toward the door gave him a bit of confidence when he didn't get better acquainted with the floor.

A cool blast of air wrapped itself around Marshall, and he took a moment to relish it. He could hear the unmistakable sound of Clint's diesel dually parked at the curb. A fortifying breath filled his lungs, and Marshall stepped out into the openness of the lonely world.

He jerked open the door, and Clint said, "Take 'er easy there, pardner. This isn't the bathroom door you're swinging open." Clint reached a helping hand over the center console, and Marshall tried to focus more on getting up into the truck instead of the tingling sensation of Clint's flesh pressed against his own.

Marshall settled in, fastened his seatbelt, and rolled down the window. Clint shifted the truck into gear, and they sped down the street. Within minutes, the poorly lit streets of the small town receded into the background. Marshall stretched his hand out the window. The wind pressing against his flesh occupied his mind. It wasn't until Clint asked, "What did you say?" that he realized he'd been muttering the words to Patsy Cline's *Crazy* under his breath.

"Did you say you're crazy for loving me?" Clint asked.

Marshall pulled his gaze from the grandeur of the Milky Way spread across the black sky overhead. He wanted to say a few curse words. He wanted to profess his undying love for Clint. He wanted to push these feelings so far down into his soul that it would seem like he'd never experienced them.

"Just a song. I'm drunk, Clint. I'm just…stupid drunk." He turned back to the window.

"Marshall, what the fuck is going on? You've been kinda, well, I don't know what. You're just not yourself." Clint reached over and grabbed Marshall's shoulder. Marshall pulled away and slid closer to the door. "What's wrong?"

"Nothing. Just, just pull over. I think I'm going to be sick."

Before the dually came to a stop, Marshall was out of the door and stumbling off the dirt road. A field of milo stood at the edge of the headlights' halo and stretched into oblivion. The thought to run into the rows of grain flitted across his drunken mind, but the sound of Clint's boots in the tall grass nearby quelled it.

"You need to puke?" Clint asked.

"No. Air. I need air. And space. And, and I need to…"

Clint stepped close and tried to put his arm around Marshall's shoulder. "What's wrong?" he demanded when Marshall jerked away.

The words burned the tip of Marshall's tongue—*I love you.* They would be so easy to utter. He could unburden himself, find freedom. But at what cost? Marshall pressed his back to the truck and slid to the ground. He buried his face in his hands.

"You're starting to freak me out a little bit," Clint said. "Why don't you—"

A deep rumbling that shook the ground drowned out the rest of his question. As one, he and Marshall looked up into a blinding flash of white light.

† † †

When his eyes first opened, Marshall thought he was lying in the back of Clint's dually. Unyielding metal caused pressure points on his back that led to pain and stiffness. Dull purplish-blue lighting overhead helped him realize he wasn't outside or in the back of the truck. A deep grunt forced itself out of him as he sat up. Joints popped and ached, but dismissed them the same way he did after every bender.

The room was about the size of his bedroom, but instead of being covered by bull riding photos and awards, the walls were a stark grey. They blended into the grey floor and ceiling. Everything in the room matched, except Marshall and Clint, who lay on a similar slab of metal a few feet away.

It wasn't until he saw Clint's naked body that Marshall realized he didn't have any clothes on either. His gaze roved over Clint's perfect body. From sturdy, well-muscled legs, to his dick, to his hirsute washboard abs and barrel chest, Clint appeared to be a well-carved statue. With the exception of his farmer's tan, Clint's alabaster skin appeared to be flawless. Marshall swallowed the lump in his throat and forced himself to look away long enough to get himself under control.

On wobbly legs, Marshall shuffle stepped his way across the short distance and softly called Clint's name. Clint scrunched his eyes and slowly opened them to look up at Marshall. He sat up with greater ease than Marshall had managed and dangled his legs over the side of the slab. He started to say something, but a hollow voice filled the room and cut him off.

"Good morning. You are well. Please do not be alarmed."

"Who are you?" Clint asked.

At the same time, Marshall asked, "Where are we?"

"My name is not pronounceable in your Earth language. You are on my ship. We are in orbit of the planet you call Mars."

Clint and Marshall stared at each other.

"Do not be concerned. You will be returned to your planet. First, I wish to observe you and your relationship dynamics. Would you please make love to each other so that I may record and document your behavior?"

"We're...not gay," Clint said. Marshall thought he heard uncertainty in the words.

"But the one named Marshall said that he was crazy for loving you. His conversation with the one named Lucy in your human drinking establishment led me to believe that he would not disclose his love for you. However, he did so, and it caused him distress. Is your relationship a volatile one? I have observed this in other humans."

"I don't know what you're talking about!" Marshall shouted. He ran to one of the walls and pounded on it with his fist. "Stop this. Take us back home. You have no right to do this to me. Stop it!"

"You are upset. I apologize. I am adjusting the atmosphere in the room to facilitate a state of calm. Please, breathe deeply and attempt to relax. This should only take a moment."

Marshall leaned his head against the wall and whispered curses at it and himself. Within seconds he felt his heartbeat slow, and his breathing became more regular. The adrenaline that had coursed through his veins, prompting him to get as far from Clint as he could and to shut up the alien's words, dissipated. Still, he felt Clint's gaze boring a hole in his back.

"You are now calm. Please, commence with making love."

"Is it true?" Clint asked. "Do you love me?"

"First, would you be this calm if some alien wasn't pumping this room full of chemicals?"

"I don't know," Clint said. "Maybe. Here's the thing, Marshall, I suspected you might be gay."

Marshall turned around and walked back to the slab he'd been laying on earlier. He couldn't bring himself to look at Clint when he asked, "Then why didn't you say something?"

"I didn't think it was necessary. I don't care that you like dudes or dick. Maybe I would have been a little weirded out if I knew that you love me."

"This is why I didn't want to tell you." Marshall stopped beside the slab. He pressed his hands against the smooth, flat surface, grateful that he had a barrier between him and Clint. "But I also had to tell you. It was just getting too big of a secret to hold back."

"Then why did you tell Lucy that you wouldn't say anything?"

"She's afraid that I would get hurt."

"By me?" The pain in Clint's voice stung as much as if he'd used a fist to hit Marshall in the stomach. "I would never hurt you."

"I know. I don't think she meant physically. Hell, maybe she did. Mostly I think she just meant my feelings."

"This is fascinating. I have never witnessed this part of a love making ritual. Please, continue."

Clint chuckled. "I never knew making love to a man entailed so much talking."

Marshall smiled. "It's not the best part of the experience."

"Is that so?" Clint moved to the opposite side of Marshall's barricade. He slowly reached out to place his palm on the back of Marshall's hand. "Now I know. Nothing bad has happened."

"Still wondering if that's because of the chemicals."

"The atmosphere in the room has been at Earth norms for approximately two point two five minutes. If you would like for that to be changed, you need only request it."

"We're fine," Clint said.

Marshall closed his eyes. The feel of Clint's hand on his was as electrifying as it had been last night while climbing into the truck. Sure, they'd touched many times, but that was usually just a clap on the back before the gate was opened and a bull carried one or the other out into the arena. There was no denying that this was more intimate.

He finally allowed himself to look at Clint. Those brown eyes captured his soul the way they always did. Marshall groaned and reached up. His hand slid along Clint's trimmed beard. He brushed his thumb against Clint's ear and then moved to grip his neck. Applying the tiniest amount of pressure, he leaned in and urged Clint to do the same. Marshall closed his eyes. His heartbeat increased; he could hear it in his ears.

Marshall clenched his eyes tighter. The distance between his and Clint's lips could be closing, or Clint could be preparing to knock him on his ass. He'd come this far. He'd bared this much of his soul. There was nothing left to do but take the plunge and hope that if things went badly that he could blame it on alien atmospheres and experiments gone wrong.

Clint's lips touched his, and Marshall stopped. He felt like he had to let Clint take the lead. He tilted his head to the side and slowly parted his lips when Clint's tongue brushed against them. Clint thrust his tongue into Marshall's mouth. Both men grabbed onto each other's head and took the first tentative steps to knowing each other more than they had.

The kiss lasted several minutes. When they parted, Marshall glanced down and saw Clint's firm erection lying on the slab. Clint looked down and then back up. A smile lit up his face and his eyes.

"So I'm guessing it wasn't terrible," Marshall said.

"Different, but not terrible." Clint leaned forward to steal another quick kiss. "So, I can tell you're trying not to spook me, but if we're going to do this, you're going to have to show me how to do it."

"Are you sure?"

"Yes and no. I don't think I could do this for anyone else, but I know you. I trust you." Another kiss. "Where do we start?"

Marshall tapped his palm against the slab. "Hop up here." While Clint followed the instruction, Marshall walked around to the other side and stood in front of his friend. They shared another passionate kiss. Marshall's hands traveled over the muscles of Clint's arms and chest. His fingers entwined in the course hair covering Clint's torso.

He broke their kiss and moved his lips along Clint's neck. Clint's nipples stood erect above the tufts of hair on his chest. Marshall playfully nipped at each one and kissed away the lingering traces of sensual pain he left behind. Clint's hands brushed over Marshall's arms, back, and head. He whispered his pleasure.

Marshall kissed a line down the middle of Clint's abs. He gripped Clint's waist and dragged his tongue over the long hardness that had tempted him for so long. A trail of saliva coated the underside. The sweet taste of precome encouraged Marshall, and he swallowed Clint to the root.

"Holy shit!" Both of Clint's hands moved to Marshall's head. He held his friend in place and moaned in time to Marshall's subtle up and down movements. "This is amazing."

Marshall backed off. He had to press against the resistance of Clint's hands, but only briefly. Once he was able to draw in enough air, he swallowed the thick shaft again. He'd longed for this moment. Now that he had it, now that he had Clint, he wanted to give Clint the best experience of his life.

After several times of bob-breathe-swallow, Marshall stood up. He stroked Clint's cock and kissed him. This time he pressed his tongue into Clint's mouth and let him savor the sweet taste of himself. Clint thrust upward into the tight confines of Marshall's hand and sucked on the tongue that invaded his mouth.

"Goddam, Marshall. You're so fucking good," Clint said through deep breaths.

"We're only getting started." Marshall laid his chest on the slab beside Clint. He thrust his ass out and reached back to slap it. The resultant *thwack* echoed throughout the room.

"Are you sure?" Clint asked. Marshall could hear the reserved excitement in his voice.

"If you don't fuck me I'll probably die," Marshall said. "Besides, I'm pretty sure it's the only way they'll let us go."

"Indeed. Please continue. We have not witnessed two males engaging in love making before. It is…intriguing."

"Well, who am I to deny our alien overlord?" Clint hopped off of the slab and moved behind Marshall. He rubbed his hand over the red spot on Marshall's ass before slapping it himself. The color darkened, and Marshall moaned. "Oh, you like that, huh?" Clint struck a second time.

Marshall moaned and gripped the far edge of the slab. He arched his back as much as could to thrust his ass upward in invitation. Clint continued to spank him, and Marshall stroked his own dripping cock. Nobody had ever given him exactly what he wanted. Knowing that it was his friend, his love, who paid attention to that small detail, heightened the experience.

Too soon, though, Clint stopped. Marshall felt fingers slide along his cleft. A cool dollop of spit landed at the top, near his lower back, and Clint worked the saliva down and onto Marshall's hole. When Clint's lips brushed the hot spot on Marshall's ass cheek, Marshall thrust backward. Clint's finger slipped inside. Marshall clenched and relaxed his ass, drawing the digit deeper inside.

"So tight," Clint whispered. "Can't wait to fuck you."

"Then fuck me," Marshall begged.

"Soon. But first…"

Marshall felt Clint's beefy, strong hands pull apart his ass cheeks. Another moan echoed through the room when Clint dragged his tongue across the spit-soaked hole. In a million years Marshall never thought his friend would take that plunge. Clint's beard dragged against the tender flesh inside Marshall's cleft with each stroke of his tongue. Marshall jerked himself faster.

Clint grasped Marshall's cock and pulled it down and back. He sucked a large bead of precome from the head and glided his tongue along the shaft, over the balls and taint, and then back into the wet trench of Marshall's ass. He repeated the action several times, going slower with each pass, until Marshall lay flat against the slab. Marshall lay in place, the slab gripped so tightly his fingers hurt, and enjoyed the attention.

Clint's released Marshall's erection and stood up. Marshall looked back over his shoulder and watched the long, thick hardness of Clint's dick sliding upward through his cleft. He rocked back and forth. Clint leaned forward, and Marshall came up to meet him in a kiss. Their tongues danced in each other's mouths. Clint slowly backed his crotch away from Marshall's ass. With one hand, he guided his cock toward Marshall's eager hole.

"Give it all to me," Marshall managed to say between kisses.

A bowl materialized on the slab beside them. Clint dipped his fingers into the pearlescent goop and slathered it onto his cock. His fingers slid easily inside Marshall, depositing the remainder of the alien lubricant.

"Get ready," Clint whispered.

"I've been ready. Fuck me."

Clint thrust forward. The head of his dick entered Marshall, followed by the rest of his shaft. Clint didn't stop until their flesh was pressed tightly together. Marshall clutched the slab and cursed. He'd never been so full so quickly, but the painful pleasure radiating throughout his entire body was intoxicating. He milked Clint's dick.

"So amazing," Clint said. "So amazing and tight. I'm not going to last long."

"I don't care," Marshall said.

Clint pulled out all but the head of his prodigious cock and thrust back in. He gripped Marshall's hips and held tight. Sweat dripped from him onto the floor and Marshall. Each time he bottomed out, he grunted, louder each time, until he became lost in the animalistic sound of fucking.

Marshall jerked off and encouraged Clint to fuck him harder, faster. He could feel his balls tightening and drawing closer to his body. He shouted "I'm coming" seconds before he unleashed a torrent of come against the metal slab. Grunts and groans turned to a shout. He drained himself, clenching Clint's cock with each release of his seed.

Clint pressed his broad chest against Marshall's back and switched to short, fast thrusts. His teeth and tongue teased Marshall's neck and back. "I'm coming, baby."

"God, yes!" Marshall shouted. "Waited so long for this."

Clint buried himself in Marshall, standing on his tip-toes to get deeper inside. His orgasm shook them both. Clint bit down on Marshall's shoulder and bucked wildly. Spent, he thrust a few more times and then slid out of the warm tight confines of Marshall's well-fucked ass. Gasping for breath, he slid to the floor and lay on his back.

Marshall stood up and smiled down at Clint. "Jesus, I've never been fucked like that. You're so goddam amazing." He kneeled down, and they shared a brief kiss.

"You're amazing," Clint said. "I wish you had said something to me sooner."

"Yeah, well…"

"Thank you. This data will be invaluable to my people. Please, rest. We will return to Earth soon."

The room filled with a bright white light, and Marshall slumped onto the floor beside Clint.

When he awoke, Marshall sat on the ground where he had been when the bright light first appeared. Clint kneeled beside him, his hand lightly squeezing Marshall's neck.

"Was, was that a dream?" Marshall asked.

"If it was, then I need to fuck you again to make it real," Clint said.

Marshall laughed. "You know, I've always wanted to see you wearing those black leather chaps and nothing else."

"Anything you want." Clint pulled him into a kiss.

Pheromones

By J.C. Quinn

Raimie is only visible from the chest down, the rest of him hidden in the low maintenance panel. A rainbow of wires curls around his slim chest. His white t-shirt rides up, showing the hollow of his hip bone disappearing into his cargo pants. A light dusting of silver-blue fur softens the lines of his abs. His feline tail comes up between his legs and swishes lazily in the air over his knees.

I clear my throat and look up at the flickering lights. He doesn't respond.

"Raimie," I say, stealing a glance down at him.

Still nothing.

I tap his paw with the tip of my boot. "Raimie!"

He scoots out. His shirt slides up more, showing his ribs. I step back and look down at the space between our feet as he pulls earbuds out of his scruffy, pointed ears.

"Hey, Simon. What's up?" His thin tongue and Mhurvian accent clip the consonants and draw out the R's.

"That's not how you should address me. I'm your superior officer." I glance right and left, but the hallway is empty. I could just make out the door to the left with glowing warning tape used by maintenance.

Raimie smiles. "Sorry, *Lieutenant Commander* Costello of the *USS Peithos*. How can I, a lowly engineer, help you?"

I bite my tongue and swallow my annoyance. "You need to answer your comm."

He raises his wrist and taps the cracked screen of his databand with the claw of his index finger.

"Oops." He shrugs. "I was trying to modify—" he sees something in my expression, probably frustration, and stops. "I broke it. I'll get it replaced immediately after this." His smile widens and turns apologetic, showing the tips of his fangs.

The smell of sweat and new electronics seems suddenly overpowering. I remember hearing or reading once about Mhurvians and their ability to charm. It took humans an embarrassingly long time to figure out the Mhurvians were emitting pheromones. I wonder if that's what he's doing now. *No*, I tell myself. *That would be inappropriate.* I turn and walk away before I can commit this image of him lying on the ground like that—legs open and icy blue eyes looking up at me—to memory.

† † †

Raimie is sitting across the table from me in the galley. There are other tables. Bigger tables. Lots of other people sitting and laughing and drinking with each other in the cool light. But he's here. Strands of electric blue hair have come loose from his ponytail, and he keeps tucking them back. He's the only Mhurvian on board and it tends to draw others to him. A couple girls from engineering and a nurse from sickbay are fawning over him and talking to him like they're tourists.

This was supposed to be a relaxing night off. Now I'm just putting all of my energy into not looking directly at him.

"Don't you think?" Chell says, grinning widely at me.

Shit.

"What?" I say, taking a drink of wine. Hoping she'll think I'm tipsier than I am and it will excuse the fact that I haven't been listening to her.

She laughs. Her voice is coated with cola and rum. "Never mind." She turns her attention back to Raimie. "So," she almost purrs and I can't help thinking it's a pale imitation of what he does. "Which way do you swing?"

He raises both eyebrows in confusion. "I'm sorry?"

Some of the others giggle conspiratorially.

Chell leans forward on the table. "You know. Like, Costello here."

My heart stops.

"He," she continues, "swings both ways. He likes men and women."

I cough, trying not to choke on the wine.

"Oh!" Ramie says. "You only have two sexes?"

Everyone but me laughs. I'm watching Raimie's mouth, the way his lips make the shape of words and his tongue grazes the sharp points of his teeth. Then I realize he's watching me too.

Something brushes my leg. I startle and look to find Raimie's tail curling around my calf. I try to flash him a glare, but the wine has gone to my head. One corner of his mouth quirks into a smile and I realize my face hasn't cooperated. It's gone and sent entirely an entirely different message.

† † †

We're in the lift on the way to my quarters. Raimie is standing next to me with his arms crossed, watching the holographic numbers above the door go down. A woman in a navigation uniform is front of us, looking over something on a clipboard. Raimie seems to think that's funny and curls his tail around my thigh when she's not looking.

I stand still and quiet, fighting back the desire to have my hands all over him for just a few more minutes until—

"Crew quarters; deck twelve," the smooth, robotic voice announces.

Raimie's tail slips away from me and swishes suggestively as he walks ahead of me. I stumble forward, body-checking the woman. She gives me a glare and I mumble an apology without taking my eyes off him.

"Do you know where you're going?" I ask.

"Your place, right?" He looks over his shoulder.

"You know where it is?"

He shakes his head, still smiling. I wonder if his mouth knows how to do anything else. We're alone in the hall and it's not much farther, so I grab his hand and rush to my room.

The auto-door whispers open and we fall in, his tail going under my shirt, tickling my ribs and brushing my nipples. I think about stopping him to say something about the impropriety of this whole situation. But then his mouth is over mine, massaging out the worries with his tongue. He tastes like the mint julep he was drinking. The useless knowledge part of my brain tells me that catnip is in the mint family, so he's probably high in addition to drunk.

His sweat—sharp and musky—is all around me again. My dick, already feeling cramped, twitches. I find the bottom of his standard issue t-shirt and pull it up over his head. In the simulated moonlight of my room, he shimmers. I push him and we stumble through the small quarters over to the rumpled bed.

"Oh, naughty boy," he says as I land on top of him. "I expected you to be the type to make your bed every morning."

"I guess you don't really know much about me." I unbutton his pants as his tail slithers around my leg like a snake.

He arches his back to let me pull them off. For a moment, I'm not sure what I'm looking at. The space between his legs is smooth with the same silvery dusting of fur as the rest of his body. Reading the confusion on my face, he pulls me close with his soft hands, the tip of his tail flicking across my balls.

His voice is low and rumbly. I feel the vibrations more than I hear the words. "You already have what you're looking for."

"What?" I breathe.

He grins and nips at my jaw. "You've had it all day."

I pull back. "What?"

He laughs and his hands go to my belt, making quick work of getting rid of it. His tail curls up my thigh and circles my dick.

I moan and the sound turns into realization. "Oh, wait, your penis is your tail?"

He nods.

"That's... oh, is that sanitary?"

"Is that the conversation you want to have right now?"

I try to focus on what I'm saying. Not the way his voice sounds like heavy cream or how it feels as he slowly constricts and releases my dick.

"Uh-uh," I finally manage. A second flash of realization hits me and I push him back on the mattress. "You've been rubbing your dick on me all day? That's... that's sexual harassment!"

He takes hold of the front of my shirt and pulls me down on top of him. "Shut up."

With the third realization, I understand that the smell isn't just his sweat. It's pheromones. As if he can sense my sudden trepidation, he wraps his arms and legs around me. His tail still working at my cock. The smell recedes and I miss it more than I expected to.

"Do you want me to go?" He asks, breathily.

No. I definitely don't. Even before the pheromones, I wanted this. I kiss him softly and stand up, kicking off my pants. His tail uncoils from my dick and he gets on his hands and knees. I grip his hips and thrust in hard.

A purr vibrates through his body and he arches his back. His tail runs up and down the cleft of my ass of a few times. I reach back and catch it. The fur is softer than I expected, like down feathers. The tip is moist and dripping pre-come.

I bring it to my mouth, licking away the salty drop before taking it into my mouth. His tail fills my mouth. It's rigid, but forgiving. I take it in as deep as I can, feeling it hit the back of my throat.

Tangling my fingers in his hair, I pull him up and back, against me. My skin feels electric and sparks everywhere he touches me. His moans come out in soft vibrato. I keep a firm grip on his hair, holding him close. He feels and tastes like sweet, wet velvet.

The tips of my fingers and toes tingle and buzz. I want this to last longer, but his sudden spray of hot come down my throat pushes me over the edge.

The Hidden Ones

By Gio Lassater

Doctor Darren Selby erected a force field around the crumbling stone column and remotely activated his visual recorder. He hoped it would prove to be a Rosetta stone for a dialect of the Besoc royal language.

"How long until the next quake?" Darren asked.

Beside him his Besocan guide, Astan, tapped information into his handheld computer. "We have approximately four hours before the next scheduled quake. It is supposed to be a minor one—they're just bleeding off some residual energy from a mining operation to the south. We should be fine." His beak, which extended less than two inches from his face, clacked lightly while he spoke.

If asked what the aqua-feathered alien had just said, Darren wouldn't have been able to repeat even a few words of it. The hieroglyphs etched into the stone in the center of the dig site completely engaged his mind. Quakes only concerned him because he didn't want the cave's ceiling high above to come crashing down on a find that could never be repeated in a hundred lifetimes.

"Astan, what does this symbol mean?"

Darren looked up at the taller alien and moved a step away in order to minimize neck pain from looking up so far. Astan's blue-green wings, folded neatly on his back, twitched the way they always did when he was concentrating on a task. Darren was fascinated by the appendages, which were now nothing more than another indicator of an avian ancestor.

"I'm afraid that I don't recognize that one." Astan leaned closer to the stone and traced the glyph with one of three fingers on his right hand. "It is similar to a symbol used by the Second Eyrie, but I cannot be certain they have similar meanings."

"What's the meaning you know?" Darren asked.

Astan leaned back and looked down at him. "It means 'those who are hidden.' It was applied to the unseen monsters of the night, superstitious nonsense that ended long ago."

Darren moved back in front of the column. He brushed against Astan's abdomen. The soft downy feathers on alien's well-muscled stomach caused him to inhale sharply.

"May I make a series of observations?" Astan asked.

"Certainly."

"I noticed last night that you and your colleague, Dr. Park, were engaging in sexual intercourse with one another. You appeared to be enjoying it very much. Counting this most recent occurrence, you have managed to make physical contact with some portion of my body on seven distinct occasions. If you are curious about Besocan anatomy or physiology, you are welcome to openly examine me or my penis. If you simply desire to have sex with me, all you have to do is ask," Astan said. "I believe it would sate the human condition you called curiosity."

Darren fought against the embarrassment that turned his face red. "Um, no, that's fine." He coughed and moved closer to the pillar in an attempt to escape his shame.

"I have offended you," Astan said. Darren could hear the confusion in his voice. "Forgive me. I forget that you humans are not always as forward as my species is. Would you now prefer a different guide be assigned to you?"

"No! That is, I mean, there's no need for that."

Darren started to turn around when the floor of the cavern began to shake. His feet shifted one way, and his upper body went another, landing him directly into Astan's arms.

"I thought you said four hours," Darren shouted over the noise of falling rocks and rumbling earth.

"There is obviously a problem with the seismic inhibitor grid." Astan picked him up and ran toward the square metal-reinforced structure that housed their equipment and sleeping quarters. "We will activate the force field, and I will contact Central Command to determine what has happened."

As the alien ran around falling stalactites and crumbling stone edifices thousands if not millions of years old, Darren stared helplessly behind them at the last vestige of the first Besocan people. The find of a lifetime could be reduced to rubble if the portable force field generator failed or became damaged. He swallowed his disappointment and tried to focus on caring about not dying. Darkness descended upon them as lights placed throughout the cavern met an untimely demise.

Inside the building, Astan set him down and used the communication panel to contact his government. Darren activated an energy shield that surrounded the entire structure. He moved away from the entrance and collapsed into a chair, grateful when the ground stopped moving.

Astan interrupted his attempts to wallow in self-pity and loss a few minutes later. "The main grid has gone offline. They are attempting to determine a cause. I have been informed that the mouth of this cavern has collapsed. A rescue party is on its way, but it may be several days before they can get to us."

"Don't you see that I don't care about that?" Darren shouted. He jumped to his feet and pointed in the direction of the column. "An important piece of your history is probably lying in hundreds of pieces not thirty feet away. How can you not be affected by that?"

"I am neither a historian nor a scientist," Astan said. "I am a guide, a protector. That is what I do and all I care about. You are safe, which means that I have accomplished my task. That is enough for me."

"Well, it's not enough for me, damn it. I've spent ten years on this planet, and when I finally find something worthwhile, it gets destroyed." He stalked to the sleeping area and threw himself onto his cot. "Wake me up when it's safe. I don't want to face the possibilities right now...or see your uncaring face."

† † †

Darren slowly opened his eyes and rolled onto his side to look at the rest of the building. The ground was thankfully still, but he could hear a high-pitched sound, almost like a buzzing, coming from somewhere outside.

"Astan, do you—" He realized the alien was gone.

Hurtling the cot beside him, he rushed to the entryway and stared out at the cavern. The barrier had been deactivated, and dust from outside had slowly begun to drift inside. Sticking his head out, he looked slowly from side to side.

Even with the lights destroyed, bioluminescent moss and other light-bearing plants gave the entire area a faint purplish-blue glow that let him see a few feet away. Great piles of rubble and debris surrounded him on all sides where once stone pillars had grown from floor to ceiling.

"Astan! Astan, where are you?"

His voice reverberated throughout the cave, but once it died out only silence replied. With his luck Astan had most likely gone outside to survey the damage, slipped, and dashed his head open on a rock. He had no idea why he automatically assumed the worst, but he attributed it to his feelings about the stone pillar's potential destruction.

If the contents of the building had been jumbled about due to the earthquake, Astan had set them straight before leaving. Darren found his handheld computer and the first aid kit. He grabbed a bottle of water and strapped a light to his wrist before heading out.

There was no way of knowing which way his guide had gone. He was most likely near the caved-in entrance, but Darren decided to go the other way. He felt selfish and embarrassed to be going back to the stone pillar. Astan could be hurt or dying, but he had to see for himself if the expedition was a total loss.

The run from pillar to building had taken Astan only a matter of seconds due to his athleticism, strength, and speed. However, he hadn't had to deal with rocks and boulders littering his path. Climbing slowly over a huge chunk of stone that glittered in the beam of his light, Darren slid down the other side and walked through a minefield of smaller debris.

As he got closer to his destination, the buzzing intensified. He stopped, realizing he had become so accustomed to the noise that he had forgotten about it. Since it had gotten louder, though, he could feel it racing along his nerves like a fire that could not be extinguished.

The closer he came to the pillar, the louder the noise became until he thought his eardrums would rupture. Sitting atop the remains of a stalagmite, he pulled two pieces of what passed for gauze among the Besocans from the first aid kit and shoved them into his ears. Not the most effective means, but the dampened sound no longer drove him as painfully crazy as it had.

As soon as he stood up, the noise stopped. "Of course," he said. He rolled his eyes and waited a few seconds before pulling the obstructions from his ears.

Bright light filled the cavern, forcing him to cover his eyes with his hands. Still he could see radiance—now tinged red from the blood in his fingers. After a few minutes, the light fell to a level that reminded him of a sunshiny spring day on Earth.

When he opened his eyes, he saw the light emanated from the pillar and its hieroglyphics. It stood as it had been before the quake. He laughed and jumped down from his rocky perch. The rest of the way was easily traversed, and when he stood in front of his greatest find, he realized tears raced down his cheeks.

"Dare-in."

He spun around. The voice, which had come from Astan, sounded like a myriad voices inside a great hall. The enormity and age of them weighed on him and his relief at seeing the alien alive—even though he had seemingly come from nowhere—was tempered by a sudden uneasiness.

"Astan, what's wrong?" The urge to run grew to the point he almost couldn't ignore it. "Are you okay?"

The alien tilted his head to the side, blinked rapidly for several seconds, and then stepped forward. His arms moved from his sides upward toward the ceiling, and his wings unfolded. They stretched out perpendicular from his body. The sight reminded Darren of a statue of Horus.

"The Astan is still here, Dare-in. However, we inhabit its body now. We share its consciousness and know all that it knows." He stepped around the human and placed his hands flat against the glowing pillar.

Darren heard the chorus of voices chanting in a chirruping language he had no hopes of understanding. "Who are you?"

Astan looked at him without breaking contact with the pillar. "We are the Hidden Ones. We are the first to inhabit this planet. Long before the Besocans descended from their lofty nests, we called this planet home. We have come to reclaim that which is ours and to guide our children into their future."

"Astan said the Hidden Ones were a superstition," Darren said.

Suddenly the light from the pillar died out, and Astan fell to his knees. His hands slid along the stone and rested on his head. Darren could see him breathing deeply, heavily. His body pulsed with green energy that roiled beneath the feathered skin before it began to crack and slough off.

Without thinking, Darren rushed forward. "What's happening? You're going to kill Astan. You have to stop!"

"Stand back, Dare-in. The Astan will not be harmed." As he spoke, feathers and flesh rained onto the floor or disintegrated in beams of light that punched outward from various spots on his body. When the last trace of his Besocan self fell away, he slumped to the ground.

Darren stared in awe at the creature lying before him. Where before Astan had been blue feathers and wings, now he had silvery, fleshy skin stretched over muscles. Short, spiky hair had pushed upward from his head and in a line down the middle of his back. His wings were nowhere to be seen, but where they had connected with his back were soft, circular tufts of blue hair.

He attempted to stand, but fell back onto his knees. Darren reached out to steady him. Astan wrapped his arms around the human, pulled him close, and rested his head against Darren's stomach.

"We are weak. The transformation is taxing for us. The Astan's body was not meant to undergo this change." He took a deep breath and released it in a shuddering spasm. "We need energy."

Darren looked at the stone pillar. "Can you take it from there?"

"We have used the battery completely." Astan looked up at Darren. "We feel the electrical impulses in your body. Your energy could sustain us."

"Whoa, hold on." Darren held his hands up and shook his head. "I'm not a battery. If you drain my energy, it'll kill me."

"We will not drain your life force. We will simply use it to reinvigorate ourselves." Astan's hands moved from Darren's back and grasped his hips. "You were intrigued by The Astan. You...touched him. He knew you wanted him to touch you. Is this true?"

Darren turned red, and Astan tilted his head to the side. "The Astan caused that same reaction from you before we did. You desire The Astan. He will give himself to you. We will utilize your energy. Are you agreeable to this?"

"What the hell! Are you asking me if I want to fuck you? All of you?" Darren pushed Astan's hands away and moved back out of reach. When the alien stood up, he couldn't help but look down. He felt himself turn a darker shade of red.

Astan lifted Darren's head and stared deeply into his eyes. "We recreated ourselves in an image you would find familiar. The Besocans are unique, and if we are to be their voice and lead them into the future, humans should not fear us. They should not be in awe of us."

"Well you won't get any complaints from me," Darren said.

"Will you be with us, Dare-in? The Astan will comply." His eyes lost focus for a moment before a familiar glint returned to them.

"Astan."

"Yes, Darren. The Hidden Ones need you. Will you help them?"

"Is this what you want?" Darren asked.

Astan smiled and closed the distance between them. He placed his hands on Darren's cheeks and kissed him lightly on the forehead and then the lips. "I told you, I'm a guide. I help and protect people. That is my purpose. Help me help the Hidden Ones. Please."

Darren rested his hands on Astan's chest. The soft feel of feathers was gone. Now, he felt great heat beneath his palms, mixed with a rhythmic pulsing inside the alien's body.

"Please," the chorus said, mimicking Astan's words.

"Well, it's not every day that I can have sex with an entire race all at once." Darren stood on his toes and considered Astan's new mouth. His barely-there beak had been replaced by broad, pouty lips.

Astan smiled, and Darren realized it was the first time he'd seen the alien show any expression. The gesture caught him off guard and melted away the last resistance he felt.

Grasping Darren's hand, Astan led him to the building. As he walked, piles of rubble rolled out of the way, creating a clear path for them. Darren marveled at the power the Besocan now possessed thanks to the Hidden Ones.

When they stepped into the structure, Astan asked, "How do we begin?"

"Well..."

Darren closed the short distance between them and pulled him down for a kiss. His tongue slipped between the alien's lips. At first Astan stood immobile, but when Darren wrapped his hands around Astan's quickly stiffening cock, he relaxed into it.

The pulsing within Astan's chest beat against Darren. The sensation raced through every inch of flesh that touched. Darren smiled against Astan's lips.

"What is that?"

"It is the Hidden Ones. It is us. Me." Astan kissed him again. "It is you."

"Come here." Darren led Astan to a cot and pushed him down onto it. "Relax. This is about you conserving and receiving energy. I'm going to give you all I can."

Sinking to his knees, he wrapped both his hands around Astan's cock and slowly tugged on it. The alien closed his eyes and sighed. Darren dragged his tongue over the engorged, dark blue erection. The pulsing intensified.

Darren opened wide and pressed forward, taking in as much of Aston's cock as he could. When the head hit his throat, he backed off. His tongue slithered along the bottom and swirled up and over the top. His hand tugged upward on the hard flesh, drawing the foreskin into a bunch that he could lick and nick with his teeth. Astan moaned and ran his fingers through the thick mop of Darren's hair.

Kissing his way along the shaft, Darren lifted the Besocan's legs into the air. His tongue bathed the tender flesh between balls and ass, sending shivers through Astan's body that rivaled the pulsing of the

Hidden Ones. A finger slipped into the tightness of Astan's ass, brushing gently over and around the hidden treasure within.

"Get on your knees," Darren commanded, and Astan complied.

With his ass completely exposed, Astan looked over his shoulder, watching as the human buried his face in the hard mounds of flesh. Darren watched the alien's eyes flicker back and forth from Astan's awareness to that of the Hidden Ones as he licked up and down. Astan's moans filled the room and goaded Darren on.

Soon his fingers joined his tongue, working their way inside Astan, exploring him as intimately as Darren had explored the ancient cavern outside. He wanted all of Astan's secrets to unfold before him, to welcome him inside. When he could contain himself no longer, he undid the clasp on his breeches, freeing his cock.

He spat on Astan's hole, working more and more saliva into it while stroking his own erection. It dripped with anticipation, and he had to focus himself to keep from soiling the cot. He wanted to fill Astan with his power, his essence. With two fingers inside the alien, Darren used his other hand to wipe away a drip of precome.

Astan greedily sucked the sweet nectar from the human's fingers. "Dare-in, you replenish us. Give us more."

"Gladly."

Darren stood and pulled Astan from the cot. He pressed against the solid, muscular back in front of him, bending the alien at the waist. Gripping his cock, he dragged it along the cleft of Astan's ass, occasionally pushing in to graze the wet hole Astan wanted filled.

Astan bent forward farther. One of his hands reached back, pulling his ass cheeks apart while his other hand wrapped around the edge of the cot. "Fill us, Dare-in. Give us your seed, your essence. Make us strong."

Darren pressed the head of his dick against Astan's hole and held it there. The Besocan's quivering began to draw him in, but Darren held back. He knew he wouldn't last long, and he wanted to prolong the experience. Gripping Astan's waist, Darren slowly inched forward. He resisted the urge to enter in one thrust. Slowly, painfully slowly, he allowed the head of his cock to be pulled inside.

Astan moaned. The pulsing in his body intensified. It seemed to reach through him and draw Darren forward. Before the human realized it, he was buried to his balls within the alien, unable to move. Astan's body and power took over. It surged along and through Darren's hard flesh. Darren was fucking and being fucked without moving.

The pulse traveled into his balls and up his spine until it reached his heart. His breathing became more rapid, and when Astan reached farther back and encircled his own hole with a thick finger, Darren had to fight for control. The Hidden Ones filled him with their thoughts and their essence. He felt the greatness of their age and knowledge as it poured into him to replace the energy they drew out.

When he felt their minds brush against his own, he lost control. With a primal scream drawn from millennia in the past, Darren gave in. His balls constricted, and his come flooded into Astan's ass—all without him having moved an inch. The Hidden Ones drew the hot liquid from him, and then continued until he had unleashed a second torrential flood.

Astan released his hold. Darren felt the Hidden Ones recede back into their host. He felt empty, hollow, spent. He collapsed. His lungs fought for air, even though his breathing had returned to normal. When Astan scooped him off the floor, he huddled against the spot in the alien's chest that gave him a sense of belonging in the universe.

"You have made us stronger, Dare-in. We would return the favor."

With no more effort than an animal tossing a favorite toy, Astan maneuvered Darren in his arms until the human's chest was pressed against his own. Their lips clashed, and Darren moaned into his mouth. When he felt the alien's hard cock pressing against his own eager hole, he pushed downward.

Caught up in the desire to connect with Astan again, he wrapped his legs around the alien and willed himself to open up. Initial stabs of pain and discomfort washed away when the pulsing once again filled him from the inside out. Astan's arms were everywhere, touching everything—Darren's cock, his face, his hair, a finger sliding into the already-full confines of his ass. Darren had never experienced anything like it.

Within moments he shot another load onto Astan's chest and rubbed it into the silvery flesh. Astan grunted, slammed his cock as far as it would go into Darren, and released a geyser of come. Darren screamed as the liquid rushed into him and the pulsing shot from his ass into his brain. Darkness colored the edges of his vision, and he pressed himself against Astan, holding on and riding the wave of euphoria and endorphins.

Just when he thought he would lose consciousness, he felt the Hidden Ones' presence in his mind. The pulsing abated, but their soothing voices calmed him and held him in a tender mental embrace.

"Dare-in, you have replenished us. Our transformation is complete. Now yours begins."

The Hidden Ones' voices whispered unknown words in his mind. The pulsing settled in his chest. He felt energy course through his veins. Astan's cock hardened within him again. Looking down, Darren saw a luminescent glow radiate out from his heart. When his human flesh began to melt away, revealing silvery skin beneath, he pressed his lips against Astan's and waited for the future to arrive.

Skin Deep

By Stephanie Loss

Standing in the cramped bunker, more spacious now with only bare pallets to furnish it, I could hear the shuffling footsteps and relayed orders of my fellow crewmen unloading the last of the cargo. I listened with half an ear and gathered up my scattered belongings into my worn-in shoulder bag. I took a quick stock to ensure I had everything: hygiene essentials, some spare clothes, a deck of cards, a few lighter books, and my I.D. with the healthy amount of credits I'd managed to save up from my past few jobs.

"Hey, Jhase!"

Slinging the bag across my body, I spun to see Jat leaning one arm against the door jamb. He wiped his forehead with the back of his other arm and sighed. His chestnut skin and shaved noggin glittered under the muted lights, the front of his shirt already soaked through. His pine-colored gaze prickled along my skin, glaring an accusation, the scar along the right side of his jaw tightening.

"You think you can weasel out of work by lollygaggin' 'bout in the barracks?"

"Just grabbing my things. Besides, we've unloaded most of it."

He grunted and swept the room one last glance. "Gonna be strange sleepin' in a real bed again. Not that I'm complainin'. I'm fucking sick'a hard-ass pallets."

"Yeah."

We took in the lifeless room for another minute, memories filling it for a moment with men and objects no longer there. Jat clapped a hand on my shoulder and turned me toward the door.

"Come on. We better help with the last of the crates, or they might decide not to pay us!"

The last of the shipment had already been hauled off and stored by the time we made it to the cargo bay. The men stood lined up for their wages while those setting out on the shuttle's ensuing trip readied the next shipment.

Jat and I held out our badges for the foreman, and I watched him close to make sure the right amount of credits got transferred. I stowed the I.D. in my shoulder bag and headed out of the loading bay. Jat followed a few seconds after.

"You gonna sign on with that job heading for Eiskar?" he wondered, pocketing his own card.

I lifted one shoulder and let it drop. "Not sure. I might just stick around here for a bit. I've got enough credits saved up to last me a few months, and I could use a break. Besides, it's been awhile since I've been home. I'm not sure I even remember where it is anymore."

Jat snorted and swigged from a small flask. "That li'l hovel you call an apartment ain't home, man. Drifters like us don't have homes." He offered the flask to me. I shook my head, and he took another sip before returning it to an inner pocket of his greasy denim jacket.

"Well, it's the closest thing I've got. What about you?"

"I know some people in town. Probably just stay with them a week or two an' then head on out again. I ain't never been out passed the H-sector. Think I'd like to see what's out there."

"Let me know when you plan to ship out."

He smirked sideways at me. "Why? You thinkin' on joining me? We take on any more jobs together, I might think you're sweet on me."

"Get over yourself, Jat."

A chuckle rumbled from his chest like rolling thunder. We stopped, and he jerked his chin straight ahead. "My contacts live over by that old theatre on Lout. Come by and visit some time."

"I'll do that."

We parted ways, Jat heading toward the city's center, and me branching off toward the gritty buildings a few blocks from the shipping quarters. No more than ten minutes passed before I reached the familiar, rundown apartment building.

The crumbling, gray-bricked monstrosity stood only four stories tall. Despite looking feeble and subdued beside the taller structures crowding it, it somehow seemed larger than I remembered it. Then again, I suppose anything would seem big after spending month-upon-month of sharing cramped bunkers with dozens of other men.

Off in the distance stood the shining heart of the city, untouched by the unseemly corrosion that afflicted the rest of the town. Here and there the perimeter ward sparkled against the darkening sky like gold pixie dust, a subtle reminder that it isn't just money separating the highbrows from the common rabble. There are ways around that, of course, but I.D. manipulation is costly. If the price isn't enough of a deterrent, the threat of Deprivation if caught keep most people in their "proper" place.

I admired the harsh disparity the crumbling buildings made juxtaposed against the glowing inner-city high-rises. A fantasy of what it would be like inside those pristine walls flitted across my mind before I shook it off. Dreams were a waste of time. Plans were what got you places, and the first thing I planned to do was shower until the water ran cold.

The hinges squawked like a banshee when I pushed past the front door, and my footsteps sent a hollow echoed against the peeling wallpaper. Dust drifted in lazy circles in my wake before settling back down to the perpetually grubby floorboards. Ignoring the protests of the staircase, I made my way up to the top floor.

† † †

The pipes rattled when I flipped on the water, the first of the spray brown with rust. I let the water flow until it ran clear and steamy before jumping in.

The shower was as rundown as everything the dumpy apartment had to offer, but the water was hot and the pressure decent—about the only saving grace the place could boast of. The knot that had been building in my left shoulder since signing on with this last job began to melt away under the beating droplets.

I took my time, savoring the crisp scent of soap as dirt and sweat sloughed off. I threaded my fingers through my hair and realized it had grown much longer since the last time I'd been home, the sepia waves reaching down to tease my shoulders. My hands moved down, relearning arms that were ropier than before underneath a collage of interlocked images. The glowing flowers of Kyel wove themselves between the blue, tiny, cat-like creatures that are abundant on Drolecth. The ornately detailed religious buildings of Gaia, where my people originated but which we outgrew, bled into colorful landscapes of every hue imaginable, melding together in a mish-mash of color. Lastly I took in the faces, each belonging to individuals who had touched my life. The memories brought a smile to my face as I looked them over, following my fingers over my arms and across my chest before continuing further down to the trail of hair on my abdomen, where the ink stopped.

I cleaned lower and my breath caught. Lathering more soap, I palmed my half-formed erection. With a sigh of relief I sank against the shower wall, ignoring the grime to focus on the familiar tingle in my shaft. I stroked calloused fingers lightly up and down my length, a slideshow of the men I'd worked with these last few jobs flashing across my mind. Privacy is hard to come by when you share living space with more than twenty other men. It's a kind of blissful torture, being constantly surrounded by half-naked men and unable to do more than admire from afar, not even the comfort of a quick jerk to ease the constant ache.

One of my bunkmates sprung to mind in particular—Gehker—a new recruit to the circuit and less muscular for it. He was on the newer side of manhood, no more than twenty-two, and so still held that bright-eyed wonder and untamable excitement for new experiences I remembered from my first trips. Maybe that is what had intrigued me about him. Whatever the reason, I found myself watching him more than the others, wishing so many times for a chance to sneak him off away from the others, for five minutes of whatever he'd be willing to give me. I could practically smell his breath in my face, taste the salt of hard labor on his dewy, dark skin, feel myself lift him like a crate and pound him into the ship's metal walls...

My stomach clenched, and I had to bite back a moan as two months' of neglect brought me rushing toward peak in mere minutes. Taking myself in a more firm grip, I sped up my movements until my breathing grew ragged and my body trembled on the precipice of orgasm. Groaning a curse, I aimed down at the last second, and my pent-up frustration swirled down the drain. My orgasm left me panting, drowsy, and sated, but the relief was hollow and short-lived.

How long had it been since I'd felt a touch other than my own? A year? Two? That last time had been a brief fling, just like all the others. That's the one major downside to working cargo jobs. Relationships are impossible to maintain when you ship out for months at a time.

The water had grown cold. I shut off the shower and dried myself. Wrapping the towel around my waist, I grabbed up my clothes and made for my bedroom. Tossing the bundle into the corner of the room, I flipped on the light. A small groan had me jerking my head toward the sound, where a pile of blankets moved to reveal a gray-skinned man occupying my bed. Based on his smoky complexion and mercurial hair, I figured him to be Danovian.

"Who the fuck are you?"

The stranger snapped to a sitting position, his eyes sweeping over me with shock and trepidation. "M-my common name is Talden. Who are you?"

"The guy who owns this apartment! You have two seconds to explain yourself before I call the authorities."

He held out his hands in a pacifying gesture. "I'm sorry! Kal told me I could stay here. He said that—"

"Kal?" He bobbed his head, still wary. "That slimy weasel. He's crossed the line this time." The Danovian took a cautious breath to speak, and I pointed a finger at him in warning. "I'm going to straighten this out right now. Stay here." I waited until he nodded, his shoulders slumped, then headed out into the living room, remembering to grab a pair of sleep pants on my way out. Slipping them on in a rush, I set out to hunt down my two-timing landlord.

Heading down to the ground floor, I pounded on the sleezeball's door, dust motes drifting down from the ceiling to light upon the doormat.

"Kal! Open up." No answer. I tried the handle to no avail, then pounded harder, shaking the door in its frame. "Kal! If you don't open this door—"

The deadbolt snapped into place, and the door jerked open. Kal glared at me in his doorway, his translucent orange eyes bleary with sleep and his pajamas rumpled. Much like his building, Kal appeared worse off than the last time I'd seen him. My anger dissipated briefly when I took in the new lines etched into his chalk-white face. His silver hair had receded another inch at least, which apparently got added to his waist line.

"Man, you look like shit."

His glare intensified. "You nearly bust my door in at this time of night to swap beauty tips?"

My sympathy shriveled to nothing, his tone rekindling my anger. "No. I came to ask you why I came home to find a Danovian squatter sleeping in my bed."

In a blink, he went from accusatory to guarded, gauging just how much shit he was in. "What makes you think I know anything about it?"

"He gave you up when I threatened to have him arrested."

Kal cursed in his mother tongue. He glanced around the hall before taking a cautious step back into his apartment. "Hey, uh, look. It's a bit late to get into this. Whadda ya say you come back tomorrow and—"

I slammed the door back open when he tried to close it in my face. "I can't believe you rented out my place. We had a deal, Kal. I told you I'd pay you when I got back from this last job."

He folded his arms, gaze shifting to the floor. It was the closest thing to an expression of guilt I would likely get. "Yeah, well, you also said you wouldn't be back for another couple weeks."

"So…what? You rent my place out while I'm not here while still charging me rent? I could sue you for this."

He held his palms out toward me in surrender. "Okay, look. I'm sorry, Jhase, but I needed the money. I gotta make a living too, ya know? And the kid didn't have anywhere to go! You know how folks can be. The boy's one'a my own, and I was jus' looking out for kind. You can understand that, right?"

"Save the "Good Samaritan" speech. The point is, you sublet my apartment without my permission."

"He needed a place to lay low. He was gonna be put in the Exchange, Jhase! I couldn't let that happen." I studied him for a second, trying to read in his face if he was being sincere or not. When I realized he meant it, my sympathy started to get the better of my outrage.

The Exchange is the government sanctioned species trade for rabble that aren't productive drones, but don't have the clout to live amongst the inner city wealth. It is run and regulated by the E.T.H.I.C.S.—Equality Trust Honor Innovation Cooperation Safety— Confederation, who for some reason fail to see the irony in overseeing a thriving, intergalactic skin trade network.

People from all species are Exchanged for various purposes, some more salacious than others, but those with pretty faces are often assigned as entertainment for the wealthy, in one form or another. Danovians are especially sought after due to their uncommon genetic legacy of sequential hermaphroditism—aka, being able to change between genders. The market for a sex slave that can please both the lady and lord of the house equally is a vast one amongst highbrows. I knew for a fact that Kal himself had had a run-in with the Exchange when he was younger, although his less-than-transcendent features saved him from the more debasing trades. Based on the quick glimpse I'd gotten, I had a feeling the Danovian upstairs wouldn't have been so lucky.

"That still doesn't excuse the fact that you did it without asking me first." I tried to maintain my harsh tone, but it had softened, and Kal jumped at the slip in temper.

"I'm sorry. You're right, and I'm sorry. Let me make it up to ya. How's about I don't charge you rent for the time you were gone—"

"You mean the time you were renting out my place illegally?" He made a shushing gesture and glanced around, despite the fact that no one else was likely awake. Even if they had been, the other tenants wouldn't to risk their homes by reporting Kal to the authorities.

"Yeah, whatever. Just hear me out. Just let the kid stay the next couple of weeks until he can find somewhere else to go, huh? I'll even replace that rusty rail on your balcony for ya."

"Oh, you mean the rail you should have fixed a year ago because that's your job and it's a safety hazard?" He stared at me in silence, and if a forty-something-year-old man could pull off the kicked puppy look, he managed it. I pulled at my bangs and resisted the urge to scream. "Fine!" I said, dropping my arm to my side. "Fine. But," I began before he could interrupt, "he's paying half my rent. And you will replace that fucking railing!" Kal began nodding before I'd even finished.

"Done and done. Thanks, Jhase. I owe you. I really, really do."

"You're damn right you owe me," I yelled at the door. Kal had already retreated into his apartment and drawn the bolt.

† † †

I sighed, closed the door behind me and locked it. A small shifting to my left caught my attention. The Danovian sat on the sofa, his fingers twining through his quicksilver hair. He looked over and his hands stilled, his teeth worrying his lower lip. Leaning back against the door, I examined my new roommate a bit closer.

Kal had called him a kid, but he didn't appear to be much younger than me. I'd have pegged him to be late twenties. He'd tossed on a worn, navy t-shirt that I didn't recognize. I examined the likewise unfamiliar blue and gray plaid sleeper pants, grateful at least that my closet hadn't been raided.

"What did you say your name is?"

I watched the lump in his throat bounce with a swallow. "Talden, sir."

"I'm Jhase."

He bowed his head toward the floor, twisting his hair again. "I suppose I should get my things."

My throat tightened. Seeing him sitting there, so sure that he was about to be kicked to the street, I knew that even if Kal hadn't guilted me into letting him stay, I would never have been able to go through with it.

"Yeah, you should. You're sleeping on the couch." His head shot up and he stared at me, his mouth agape.

"You mean you're—you'll let me stay?" His voice was smooth and cool, a lilted alto that was higher than most men I'd met. The wavering note of hope in it only solidified my decision.

"For the time being."

His palms snapped together, the tips of his fingers touching his forehead. "Thank you, sir! I promise, I won't be in the way."

"Stop with the 'sir' crap. I told you, my name is Jhase."

"Jhase," he repeated.

I pointed back toward my bedroom. "Go grab your stuff."

Heading back into my bedroom, he returned to the living room only seconds later with another t-shirt, red this time, a pair of well-worn jeans, and a comb. I travel light for jobs, but the paltry number of things he owned made me look like an over-packer.

"Is that all you have?"

He stood beside the couch awkwardly holding the small bundle. His feet fidgeted. He glanced around, his cheeks flushing a light plum beneath his gray complexion. "I have a toothbrush in the bathroom cabinet and some food in the refrigerator. Other than that I've been using your toiletries—but I can pay to replace what I've used!"

"Don't worry about it. You said there's food?" I paced over to where stained carpet gave way to scuffed and dingy tile. Opening the fridge, I found only bread, eggs, cheese, and milk. "Well that's not gonna last. We'll go grocery shopping tomorrow." I shut the door and turned back to him. "And we'll pick up some clothes for you while we're at it. A man needs more than one set."

Talden's cheeks deepened in hue before he tilted his head. "Why would you help me? Mere minutes ago you were furious to find me living here uninvited."

I opened my mouth to answer, but I realized that I had no idea why I wanted to help him, except that I couldn't live with myself if I didn't. Perhaps because I knew what it was like to be down on your luck. Or maybe my conscience didn't like the idea of him being condemned to a life of slavery if I could prevent it. A smaller, shallower part of my brain suggested that he was quite attractive, and it would be nice to have something pretty around to brighten up the place.

"Kal told me about the Exchange," I answered, opting for a mixed truth. "Nobody deserves to be a plaything for rich, perverted assholes. Besides, it'll be cheaper for us both to split rent."

His thin lips tilted in a gentle smile. He slipped his bangs behind one ear. "Thanks."

"Don't mention it." Neither sure what to say or do next, we stood in an uncomfortable silence that only grew worse as the seconds ticked by. Damn it! It's my apartment, and somehow I felt like the intruder. Finally, I cleared my throat and gestured at the end tables bracketing the couch.

"Feel free to keep your stuff in those. I'm turning in for the night."

"Alright."

I watched him bend to place his few possessions in the nearest table's cubby. I started to head into the bedroom when his sleep pants pulled tight across his backside, catching my attention. That quick, the pressure I'd released not an hour ago started to build again, and I had to shift away when he turned back to wish me good night.

"Yeah, see you tomorrow," I muttered. Then I fled to my room and shut the door.

† † †

The next morning, no foreman shouted for the next shift or reprimanded me for sleeping in late. So I did just that, luxuriating in the bliss of not having anything to do. When I did decide to crawl out of bed, the sun had a few hours' head start. I blinked my vision clear until I could make out the furniture in the windowless room. My blanket hung more off the bed than on me, and I let it fall the rest of the way as I sat up.

I'd slept restlessly, plagued by vivid dreams that seemed to have faded with waking. Though I couldn't recall the specifics, the graphic nature of the dreams stuck with me, and I felt mild embarrassment upon recalling that Talden had headlined in them. I blamed that on my year-or-more long dry spell and the fact that the entire bed smelled like him—or I assumed it was his scent, anyway. I could have changed the sheets the night before, but it had seemed like too much effort. What was the point in changing them when they smelled perfectly fine? Better than fine, if I was being honest.

Stop it, Jhase.

I couldn't hear rustling or anything else that indicated Talden was up and moving about in the living room, but perhaps he was a late riser. I resolved to find out, since it beat sitting in bed all day.

Blinking my way into the too-bright living room, I found Talden silhouetted on the balcony. He'd left the sliding door open, and a soft, warm breeze played through his hair and blew it back from his face. With the mid-morning suns illuminating his features, I noticed a gold ring piercing his left eyebrow. I watched him stare out across the city, and it took me a moment to realize he was staring where the golden sheen of the Inner Sanctum's wards melded indistinguishably with the light of the clashing suns.

I drew closer. The wind shifted the hem of his sleep pants and something else sparkly caught my attention: three trade coins glinted from his ankle. What at first I thought to be an anklet to match the ring in his left eyebrow, I soon realized was in fact inked into his skin. I'd never seen metallic tats before.

He didn't seem to notice my presence, so I took a few more seconds to look him over before I spoke.

"You're going to let bugs in."

Talden jumped and half-turned to where I stood taking up the balcony doorway.

"I'm sorry. I can close it."

He made to move toward it, but I held up a hand.

"Leave it. I was just kidding. Place could use some airing out."

Talden turned back to lean on the rusted railing lining the small balcony. The thing still hung on by the remaining bolts, but it was probably a strong gust of wind away from giving up the ghost and dropping on some unsuspecting lunk. Despite the danger, I found myself stepping up to lean on the rail beside Talden.

"The apartment's shit, but you can't beat the view. Only wish I could enjoy it more than a couple weeks a year."

"Kal mentioned you do grunt work for cargo drops, and that that's why you're gone for long periods at a time," Talden said after a moment.

"Yeah. Some trips are shorter, but I tend to take the longer trips because they pay more."

"So what do you do?"

"Load cargo, ship maintenance, unload cargo."

Talden nodded, thoughtful. "I traveled here as a passenger on a luxury ship. I even had my own room."

"Must'a been nice," I muttered.

Talden picked at nonexistent dirt under his nails. "It had its moments."

I glanced sidelong at the odd way he'd said that, but he pressed on.

"But I can't imagine traveling by cargo ship. So many people in such a small space, it must be cramped with little privacy. I don't know how you could do that month after month."

I thought of the small "accidental" brushes in close quarters, the musky, sweaty perfume of so many laboring bodies in confined corridors and engine rooms, and the glimpses of crewmen changing that were only partly on purpose. "It's not that bad," I mused, surreptitiously adjusting myself. "The time passes pretty fast when you're constantly working."

Talden shifted, playing with his hair again. It looked silky, almost liquid in the midmorning light. "Don't you get lonely?"

I shrugged. "The guys are generally good men. Those of us who work the same circuits become close. A friend of mine, Jat, is staying here in the city, just a few blocks over. We've worked our past four jobs together. What about you? Do you have any friends or family in the city?"

Talden shook his head. "I left my parents behind when I went into the Exchange."

I thought back for a second. "Wait, went into? Kal told me he helped you avoid it, that that's why you were staying here."

Talden's sharp eyebrows drew together, and I noticed that they slanted up on the outer edge instead of curving back down like a Tellurian's. "Avoid? I suppose that's half right. Although Kal didn't help me avoid the Exchange so much as convince me not to go back."

"Go—" I couldn't help it. I gaped at him. "You mean you escaped, and you considered going back? Why?"

"Technically I was released. That's what this tattoo indicates," he added, lifting up his pant leg to show off the image I'd spied earlier. "It is a symbol that I've paid my debt and therefore am essentially a free man." His mouth quirked, but his tone rang bitter. "Not that they didn't try to sell me off before my contract expired. Sometimes I even wish they had. I've been giving myself to the highest bidder for so long, I can hardly recall what life was like before." He sighed and lowered the cloth back down. "But one never really escapes the Exchange."

"Meaning?"

He turned and stared out at the city once more. "It's common courtesy for patrons to gift sums of money or trinkets to those they request. I proved quite popular over the years, so when I was released and sold most of them for living expenses, I had a good sum of money. Of course, I knew it wouldn't last, so I tried to find work—at first in the Inner Sanctum, then later, when I grew more desperate, the Outer. It eventually struck me that I have no tradable skills...except one. I was selling myself in the Outer ring and considering going back to the Exchange when Kal found me. Now I'm scraping by enough for food and rent, but little else."

"How old were you?" I knew no matter what he said that I wouldn't like the answer, but for some reason I felt compelled to ask.

"Ten," he choked, the word little more than a grunt. The tone had lost all semblance to the musical, high tenor from before. "My first 'client' was an official on board the luxury ship that brought me here, although he wasn't really. Never even gave a gift as is customary. When I asked if he was going to pay for what he took, he just laughed and told me I should get used to getting 'stiffed.'"

"Only a child? What about your parents? Why didn't they fight it?"

"Because I wanted to go."

My confusion must have shown on my face, because he quickly explained.

"They didn't want me to go, but the E.T.H.I.C.S. Confederation controls our water and land, and for the privilege of remaining a mostly-free planet, the Exchange claims a 'donation' of one boy and one girl each year. I volunteered to go to spare my friends. Had I known what I was signing up for...I am ashamed to say I don't know I would have made that sacrifice."

"No kid should have to make a choice like that. That's fucked up! Sex is supposed to be a nice experience. For them to be forcing kids into that—!" The words lodged in my throat, rage simmering. I'd known the E.T.H.I.C.S. Confederation in general, and the Exchange in particular, were pretty shady, but I'd never realized how much rot there truly was at the core of the Universe's great, unifying government.

My chest constricted at the shadows in his eyes. His posture slumped, his weight resting against the questionably-stable balcony railing. I tried and failed to imagine what that must have been like. I'd been young my first time, only thirteen, but that had been my choice.

My life hadn't exactly been parties and adventure like my younger self had envisioned, but from the sound of it, the High Life wasn't picturesque like I'd always imagined.

"How did you get through it?"

"You adjust. You learn to embrace it, or at least to cope. I remember how humiliated I was at first, but the last few years I felt...nothing. It was easier that way."

Talden tortured his hair more than ever as he held a staring contest with the buildings in the distance. I decided we needed a change in topic.

"So, where's home for you?"

Talden blinked back to the moment and smiled at me over his shoulder. "Far'n, all the way over in Sector Q-17. It is a vast city with flora allowed to grow freely around the buildings. You would like it there, I think. So many colors! More than you can put a name to. I haven't seen so much color since I left—aside from your stenciled skin," he added, nodding at my bare chest and arms. "What about you?"

"My parents lived in Sector E-12. They ran a little mechanic shop there, which is where I learned about ships. My older brother runs the place now. I have a sister who lives just over on Greeth. She married into the Inner Sanctum there and never looked back. I wanted to travel and see the galaxy, so I left my parents when I was old enough to sign on to a crew. They died while I was on my second assignment— accident involving a combustion drive that hadn't been properly monitored and stabilized."

"I'm sorry for your loss."

"Don't be. It happened a long time ago."

"Still, you must miss them. And your siblings."

"Never got on with my siblings, but I do miss my parents now and then." I pointed to the tattoo that held pride of place on my left pectoral, just over the heart. "This is them. 'S from a photo I used to

116

carry with me that first year on the circuit. Now it's with me all the time."

"They look happy."

"Yeah," I agreed. "Things weren't perfect growing up, but my parents did the best they could and tried to keep positive no matter how bad things got. Wish I'd inherited their optimism."

Talden tilted his head. "Why is that?"

I shrugged and looked back at the threadbare carpet just feet away. "I guess things just never seem to get any better. Not that my life's bad, but it's not what I dreamed of when I left either. The cargo men always told us stories while we repaired their ships: of the places they'd been and exciting scrapes with death; of the different species they'd met and marvelous songs and stories—all from places so different from the rock I grew up on. Nothing ever happened there, and I couldn't wait to have adventures of my own.

"The work I do isn't as glamourous as I had envisioned as a kid, but still, I do get to travel to exotic planets and meet all types of people. Look at this one here." I pointed to a city floating in a pool of water ten times its size that rested just under my right elbow. The edges of the far off embankment bled into the surrounding tats. "This doesn't do justice to the actual scale of the place, but it is huge."

Talden's eyes grew large.

"I've never seen a city surrounded on all sides by water! How does it stay up?"

"It's an island. This is the first planet successfully terraformed by the E.T.H.I.C.S. Confederation. It's in the Central Quadrant of the Grid."

"Why do you have it on your arm?"

"This is the first planet I ever visited after leaving home. My father used to preach that it was memories, not money, that make a person rich. I keep my memories close by inking them into my skin."

"Then it seems you have lived a colorful life," Talden said, his mouth angled in a wry grin.

I caught his gaze, surprised at the shift in demeanor. The uncertainty and nervous energy from before were gone, replaced with a sardonic of humor.

"I suppose you could say that." I smiled down at the image of my parents again. "Always dreamed of workin' my way into an Inner Sanctum someday. Told my parents I was gonna own the most beautiful house there that money could buy, and that the whole family could move in."

"The Inner Sanctum is full of beauty," he agreed, his voice dull. "But only a fool lets the beauty of something blind him to its dangers."

"I suppose that makes for a lot of fools then."

It made me wonder what sort of dangers he had hidden behind that perfect face. He didn't give off a manipulative vibe, exactly, but I had no doubt he'd picked up a trick or two seducing aristocrats. Then again, people tend to lower their guard around those they underestimate, and between his svelte form, entrancing, achromatic eyes, and just-this-side-of-delicate facial structure, he probably hadn't had to work too hard at it. It wasn't a wonder he'd been highly requested.

Thin eyebrows drew together as I studied him, and I noticed the way the silvery hair there almost blended in with the lighter gray of his skin when the light struck it just right. He had a slim nose, almost too small for his face, with matching thin, plum lips the only splash of color in the monochrome face. It complimented the blush on his cheeks.

"Jhase?"

"Yeah?"

"Do you like what you see?"

"I—uh…" I brought myself back to attention and looked out at the city again. "Sorry. Wasn't trying to be rude or anything."

Talden smiled. "You stare when you think I won't notice, but you keep at a distance. Why?"

I glanced sidelong at him and realized that his eyes weren't completely without color after all, but instead caught the light like prisms, refracting the colors around him. Astonishing. "What distance? We're standing right next to each other."

"True, but your body language makes it clear that you wish to do more. Don't lie, I know attraction when I see it."

Yeah, I suppose he did.

I shrugged. "You got out of the Exchange so you'd no longer have to play sex toy to a bunch of rich fuckers with more money than morals. It seems in poor taste to hit on you."

Puce lips quirked up. "You seem like a good man, Jhase."

"I try."

Talden looked unsure again suddenly, his teeth working over his lower lip like the previous night when he'd been sure he was getting evicted.

"Could I ask you a personal question?"

I snorted. "You mean the stuff we've been discussing wasn't?" He just looked at me. I rolled my eyes. "Sure. Ask away."

"What's it like to have sex...with someone you like?"

I'm sure what I'd expected him to ask, but that wouldn't have been on the list had I made one. "Uh...what?"

"You see, I've been with men and women alike, more than can be counted, but I've never truly enjoyed it. There is little pleasure to be found when you can't say no."

"So you've only had sex against your will?" I guess I should have figured that. He'd said he'd been ten when he joined the Exchange, but I couldn't imagine associating sex exclusively with rape and manipulation, pain and sadness. My experiences with sex hadn't always been worth bragging about, but I'd never been forced into it, and certainly not at such a young age.

"I wasn't 'forced' technically—well for the most part. As I stated before, I chose to enter the Exchange, but I couldn't say 'no' without going back on the agreement."

The words "and it wouldn't have mattered" hung in the air like a ship's exhaust fumes, and I felt my chest tighten again.

"Well, there was the obvious pleasure, of course...at least, once I got older."

"But as a side effect of the act, not the main point. That's not true pleasure."

"Some of my patrons cared and gave back, and some of my loyal regulars even grew to have genuine affection for me, but it was still a hollow experience. I tried, but I could never feel anything for any of them."

His expression closed, and I reached out to touch him—stroke his back, hold his hand, pat his arm. I pulled back and scratched my neglected morning stubble instead.

"Why are you telling me all this?"

"I suppose because I can?" Talden shook his head, streamers of hair dancing around his shoulders. "You're the first person I've had the opportunity to have a proper conversation with in a long time."

Talden's hand slid over mine where it had come to rest on the railing, and I locked up, breathing quickening as my cock woke up. I jerked away and took a step backward toward the living room.

"What are you doing?" It came out rough.

"You have been watching me at every opportunity, and these walls aren't so thick. I heard you last night. You groaned into your pillows and moaned my name."

"I-I..." Saying it had been a dream wasn't likely to help matters. So instead I backed up another step, only to have him follow. "I don't want to take advantage of you."

"And if I want you to?" Talden stepped forward and grabbed my hand again, pulling me close so he could nuzzle my neck. "I've never had the freedom to choose my partner. I will stop if that truly is your wish, but mine is that you will let me lie with you, and that you will share with me what sex is supposed to be like." He gazed directly into my eyes, perfect opals meeting soil-brown, and my lungs forgot what air was. "So what will you do?" he wondered, leaning close, lips a kiss away from mine. "Will you push me away? Or will you show me true pleasure?"

His face shone full of hope and lust, and the last of my doubt abandoned me, giving way to desire.

"Ah, fuck it!" Slipping one hand behind his neck, I pulled him fully to me and claimed his mouth with mine. We melted into the kiss. Reverent fingers found my back, tracing over the tattoos as if reading braille.

"You are so colorful," he whispered in wonder, tracing the myriad tattoos along my right arm. "So many beautiful places. And such an attractive canvas."

"Beauty has many forms," I agreed, admiring the pleasing effect of gray-on-gray where his hair fell about his shoulders.

"I have never seen anyone so steeped in color. My people do not traditionally ink their skin."

Puce lips dipped down to trail feather-soft over interlocking images of animals and architecture, flora and faces, repainting the images with breath and tongue and whispered words in an unfamiliar tongue. I shuddered and savored the feel of smooth fingers tracing down my arms, over my pecs and nipples, and down to faintly tickle my abs just above my pants.

Drawing his head up from its exploration of my torso, I brought us eye-to-eye. "Color is overrated."

I pulled his lips back to mine and moaned as it also brought our bodies together. Backing us toward the sofa, I sat and pulled him into my lap. Talden began a slow, deep grinding of our hips that had me panting. He kept the pace for a few minutes until I tightened my grip on his hips, urging him to go faster. He did, but not as much as I needed.

"Faster."

"Not...yet..." he huffed.

I threw my head back with a groan as his angle altered, sliding him just right along my length. "Ungh. Talden…Just like that. Don't move."

"That defeats the purpose," he teased, but I was too far gone for quips. I panted and moaned in response, letting him do whatever he wanted.

The pressure must have convinced him better than my demand had, because he sped up, his rhythm growing less controlled. One hand tugged my hair as I had his earlier while the other squeezed my bicep, he whimpered and buried his face against my shoulder.

Talden's jagged breaths tickled my neck as we both climbed, grinding faster, pulling closer. I wormed one hand down the back of his sleep pants to grope his ass. The pressure in my gut felt ready to burst. Talden broke first. A high-pitched scream caught in his throat. His body quaked against mine, warm semen wetting the front of his sleep pants.

On the verge of my own orgasm, I grunted in frustration as Talden stilled against me. A moment later I had Talden on his back on the floor. We pooled our pants around our ankles, flung his shirt across the room. His spent cock pressed between his stomach and my unassuaged erection. The warm come covering Talden was cooling fast, but it hardly registered as I leaned down to explore that expanse of flawless gray.

Tracing my lips over his collarbone, I teased along Talden's ribs just to feel him squirm beneath me. I licked up the strong line of his jaw, tasting the salt of his skin, and a groan vibrated in his chest. I'd missed this. The feel of warm skin. The taste of salt and sweat. The smell of masculine musk and spunk. The sound of ragged breathing in my ear. Masturbation could assuage the ache in my balls, but not the one in my chest. Staring down into opalescent eyes still glazed with pleasure, I realized that no planet I'd visited, however beautiful, splendid, or exotic could ever fill that void as much as this.

Talden smiled up and curved his arms around my neck and shoulders, and my already erratic pulse stuttered. "Don't you want to finish?"

"I-I—" I coughed as the words snagged, my throat like sandpaper. "Do you want to…? I-I have some oils in my bedroom…"

Talden laughed as my face grew warm. "If you are too shy, I can take the lead. After all, I am more experienced than you."

"You can't prove that."

The grin just slanted. He toyed with the sensitive skin along my spine, teasing the nerves to life. I bent over, leaning into the caress, and let out a breathy moan.

"Do you know why my kind are so sought after for the Exchange?" Talden's breath brushed my ear. "Why the E.T.H.I.C.S. Confederation has extorted our water and soil rights hostage for Danovian sex slaves?"

"No."

"This," he hissed, running his free hand down his chest.

And then I could feel it, as if he touched us both. As he moved lower, grasping his reforming erection gingerly and teasing it harder, a dual spike of pleasure shocked through my own cock, pulling a surprised groan from my lips. I stared as he smirked up at me, reveling in his power.

"Had I a mind to, I could make you come from across the room without once laying a finger on you."

I moaned as he pumped again, then hissed in a breath, my balls aching for the release they'd been denied. "Any other special talents I should be aware of?"

"One, but it's more just a variation on the theme."

I was about to ask him to elaborate when the ghost sensation on my cock was joined by several others. Invisible hands seemed to fondle my sac and tease my inner thigh while Talden rolled my nipple between his fingers and kissed my quivering belly. More of the not-hands caressed my ass and dragged nails along my spine, setting my whole

123

body alight with pleasure. I clutched Talden's shoulders, arms, and ass blindly, lost to it all.

"Enough! Please."

The ghost sensations disbanded, leaving a pleased-looking Talden kneeling before me. I hadn't even noticed him move.

"Are you done torturing me yet?"

"No, but there's always tomorrow."

I opened my mouth to say…something…but it fled my brain as he collected the semen coating his belly and spread it over my cock.

"The oils can also wait until tomorrow." He mounted me, hesitating only at the initial insertion. The heat was incredible, and he was tighter than I had expected, given his background.

Once we'd both adjusted, I searched his face for signs of discomfort but found none. And then I couldn't focus on anything but the heat and our mingled scents as he rode me. The day disappeared as stars lit up behind my eyes, our cries rising in volume as we both rocketed toward a quick, sharp peak. Talden stroked himself in a frenzy. Carnal whimpers and moans vibrated against my ear.

I clutched the arm steadying him, breathing ragged. The nails of my other hand dug into the carpet to keep from digging into him. I screamed in frustration, the pleasure plateauing just on the edge, but not quite tipping over.

"Fuck, Talden. Faster!" But Talden was lost in his own pleasure, his come painting both of our chest with a strangled groan.

I took the opportunity to switch our positions, throwing him onto his back again and pounding into him. I hit deep inside him with each thrust, and his voice rang out even after he'd finished coming. I felt him clenching his muscles around me, driving me over the edge.

"Fuckfuckfuckfuckfuck."

My eyes rolled back and my lungs locked up. I went ridged, pumping erratically. My gasping moans met his lips when he leaned up to kiss me. Beautiful, brilliant warmth followed in the wake of the sharp pleasure as my orgasm passed. I rolled onto my back beside

Talden with a satisfied sigh, too bone-weary to even haul myself onto the couch.

Talden must have too, because despite the fact that we were both hot and sticky, he settled onto my chest, and his weight felt so good I couldn't have cared less. A breeze blew through the open balcony door, and I realized we'd been in clear view of no less than four buildings the whole time. And that was suddenly very funny for some reason. I chuckled, and then let out a heartier laugh, because it felt good.

"So, this is what true pleasure is?" Talden asked sleepily from my chest.

"A taste of it, anyway."

He adjusted, resting his chin on his arms. "Will you show me more tomorrow?"

I brushed the bangs from his face, and pretended to consider it. "Maybe. But sex isn't true pleasure. Sex is just a part of it."

"If sex is not true pleasure, then what is?"

I lifted a shoulder in a shrug. "Dunno. I've never experienced it. Never had anyone stick around long enough to find out." Looking out the window at the gold haze of the Inner Sanctum, a thought struck me.

"Hey, so you've only ever been to Far'n and here, right?"

"Yes. Some of the Exchanged got sent to other planets upon request, but they kept me here."

"How would you like to travel with me?"

Talden's up-tilted eyebrows rose. "That is an intriguing offer, but I don't know that I'm cut out for the sort of work you do."

"I didn't mean on commercial cargo jobs."

Talden's his hair shimmered to one side as his head angled in thought. "Then what exactly are you proposing?"

"I've been saving up money for several jobs now. I planned to use it for rent and expenses so I could take a break from cargo drops for a bit, but there's enough there that we could buy a small craft with it.

Always wanted my own ship. And if you got any clout still in the Inner Sanctum, we might be able to swing us a couple Freelancer Passes. The drops wouldn't be as big, but we could deliver enough to turn a modest profit maybe."

"I have some pull left. Lordess Andrenda—one of my most admiring patrons—is on the board that oversees travel and work visas. I might be able to trade a favor for a favor."

I frowned at the implication in his voice. "I didn't mean that kind of influence."

"Perhaps not, but if giving myself to Lordess Andrenda one last time means I never need do so again, then it is a trade well-worth making." His expression managed to be somehow resigned, bitter, seductive, and pleased all at once. "You're not jealous, are you?" I didn't answer, and he laughed. "Well, it may not come to that anyway. Lordess Andrenda was very taken with me, but she is also a good business woman. For a tithe, I believe she would get us the passes."

Talden unfolded one of his arms, reached out, and traced a finger over the images on the inside of my forearm.

"If I agree to come with you, will you show me all of the places you have tattooed on your skin?"

"I can show you way more than that."

Talden chuckled and leaned down to kiss my chest, just below where my parents smiled up at us. The fingers teasing my skin slid down to twine with mine. "Then I look forward to it."

Maliens

By Gio Lassater

I

The sun dipped below the western Oklahoma horizon, and Dayton Fitzgerald slipped a bulky pair of headphones over his ears and turned knobs and dials on the electronic board sitting at the end of his front porch. In the near distance, four small receiver dishes pointed up at various areas of the darkening sky, panning slowly from left to right.

The dishes scanned as far as they could, so he adjusted a few knobs and sent the array in the opposite direction. With more advanced equipment he wouldn't have to do that, but that took money he didn't have. Silence taunted him through the headphones.

When he'd first started at SETI—The Search for Extra Terrestrial Intelligence—it took mere minutes for the boredom to set in. He'd wondered how in the hell he could have been stupid enough to want to work there. Even after all these years, he still wasn't fully convinced intelligent life existed in the universe, including on Earth.

Halfway through the circuit, a brief burst of static filled the headphones, which tripped the program that brought the dishes to an instant halt. Dayton waited. Ten seconds. Thirty seconds. Nothing. The computer sent the array on its way again, constantly listening.

He sipped from a bottle of Budweiser. Only then did he notice that he'd drained it. Pitching the empty into the yard, he made sure the computer was recording, removed the headphones, and went to the refrigerator.

Damn it!—this was his last beer. He twisted the cap off and sent it sailing in the general direction of the trash can. He lifted the beer in a salute to the picture of Tony and him on the counter between the cramped kitchen and the tiny living room of his mobile home.

"Here's to you, fuck head." Half the beer disappeared down his throat, eliciting a loud belch. Gonna have to watch my intake, Dayton thought, looking down at his bare, hairy stomach. Don't want to get a paunch like the old man.

His smooth hand played along his hirsute pecs, tweaking first one nipple then the other. He stared at the photograph, remembering how it had been to be in Tony's bed.

Dayton closed his eyes. Imaging that his hand was Tony's, he continued to pull at his nipples, increasing the pressure each time he tweaked them. Slowly his hand traveled down his stomach, feeling the hard ridges of his abs before his fingers forced inside his tight Wranglers. He wrapped his hand around his own sizable dick and pulled it up past the top of his jeans and rubbed it through the rough denim.

In Dayton's memory, Tony pushed his entire length into Dayton. Gripping Dayton's muscular legs, Tony wrapped them around his waist, lifted his lover from the bed, and thrust upward into him. The room filled with echoes of sweat-soaked flesh slapping together and moans of painful pleasure.

Dayton wanted desperately to watch Tony's eyes. The magnificent green irises reminded him of emeralds trapped behind glass illuminated by fire. The sensations filling Dayton overrode his ability to maintain the visual connection. He threw back his head, reveling in the feel of Tony filling him the way no one had before…or since.

He imagined Tony filling him with come, releasing burst after burst that he thought would never stop. Dayton grunted when his orgasm hit, both in his memory and in the now, and thick ropes of come splattered against his chest.

When Tony had put him back down on the bed and pulled out of him, he felt so empty. The way he felt now.

Dayton stared down at his torso and watch his spent erection retreat into the confines of its denim prison. Swigging the last of the beer, he rubbed the come into his skin and the hair covering it, determined to shower later. With the reek of sex filling his nostrils, Dayton glanced at the picture one more time and went back to his equipment on the front porch.

† † †

"Oh, for fuck sake, D, when the hell are you going to grow up?"

Dayton groaned, grabbing his head and using his fingers to pry his eyelids apart. "Whooss 'ere?" he mumbled. He willed his eyes to stay open and focus. "Jimmy, sat oo?"

Jimmy, Dayton's older brother, stared down at his half-naked sibling lying on the wooden porch abutting the mobile home. He looked out over the scraggily front yard, taking in what could have been the aftermath of a week-long fraternity kegger.

"Damn it, D! How long are you going to keep this shit up?" he asked.

"Wha' shit?" Dayton sat up, fell over onto his side and threw up.

Jimmy stepped back from the mess, checking to see if any stray chunks had landed on his Justin Ropers. "You're disgusting. I hope you know that."

"So you tell me every time—" More vomit covered the slats of the porch "—every time you come out here and pass judgment on me, Jesus."

"I'm busting my ass to help you get this damn dream of yours off the ground, and what are you doing?" Jimmy asked.

"Here we go," Dayton mumbled.

"I'll tell you what you're doing. You're out here drinking yourself into an early death. And for what? For what, D?" he shouted, eliciting a wince from his brother. "What the hell happened to you in California? You don't have AIDS, do you?"

"Yes, Jimmy. I'm a fag, and just like every other fag in the world, I have AIDS!" Dayton hung his head, waiting for the pain from his screams to die away. "I don't have AIDS, you bigoted fuck."

"Oh, that's rich." Jimmy grasped the porch railing and looked out at the four receiving dishes. "I knew you were gay before you did. I don't care what you do with your dick. I don't care who you fuck or who fucks you. I do give a damn about you, though, even when you don't." He turned a sad smile on his brother. "I really am trying to help you. You just have to help yourself."

"Is this the start of an intervention?" Dayton sat up. "Please tell me this isn't an intervention. I can't handle another one of those."

"Fuck you, D! No, it is not a goddam intervention. I learned my lesson after the third one."

"Good man." Dayton gave his brother a thumbs-up.

Jimmy started to say something but realized it was pointless. "What are the chances that you might actually look like a human being sometime soon?"

"Don't know," he said. "What are the chances you can help me tidy this dump up?"

"I'd say the chances are as good this time as they are every damn time I've helped you clean this shithole." Jimmy went inside and returned with one of the 50-gallon garbage bags he bought the week before. "You ever decide to recycle this shit, you're going to make a killing. Of course, you'll just drink it away again."

"That's enough, Jesus. You can crawl down from your cross now. I get the picture." Dayton pushed past his brother in the trailer's doorway. "I've got to piss before I get started."

"Get a shower while you're back there. You smell like the floor of a seedy whore house," Jimmy shouted at the closed bathroom door.

"Hey, can't help it that I need some relief. Not many guys beating down the door to give me any," Dayton said. "Be out in a few minutes, bro." Water splashed in the shower.

Half an hour later, Dayton looked human again, and Jimmy had five full bags stacked at the end of the trailer.

Stepping onto his porch—which Jimmy had sprayed clean— Dayton finished tucking his shirt into his tight-fitting Wranglers. "All bullshitting aside, Jimmy, I really do appreciate all that you do for me." He pulled his brother into a hug, clapping him on the back.

"What happened in California, D?"

"I'll tell you later."

"You keep saying that," Jimmy said.

Dayton scrubbed his face with his palms. "Because I don't want to talk about it. I don't want to think about it, but I do. I think about it constantly, and it eats me up."

"Just fucking tell me. It can't be that bad."

Dayton jumped off the porch and took three long strides toward his control board before he stopped and turned to face Jimmy. "Fine. You want to know what has my guts and heart twisted into a beer-soaked knot? Well, sit your ass down, and I'll tell you. Then, when we're done, you don't give me anymore shit about this. Good?"

"Good," Jimmy said.

Dayton walked back and sat on a dry spot on the porch. He stared out at some hills painted hazy by distance and took a deep breath. "His name is Tony."

131

II

Dayton stared at the message on his phone. Left work early. I think I need Dr. Fitzgerald to come triage me. He sent a quick response that he was on his way home and laid a box containing a dozen yellow roses—Tony's favorite—on the passenger seat of his car.

The wind had made a mess of his hair by the time he pulled into the driveway. He finger-combed it into a semblance of normal, grabbed the roses, and dashed to the door. Tony had already unlocked it. Dayton kicked it shut behind himself, dropped his leather briefcase onto a chaise, and strode into his bedroom.

Tony was propped up by a mountain of pillows in the center of the bed. His legs stretched toward the sides of the bed, perfectly displaying his semi-hard erection. He broke into a mischievous grin when Dayton dropped the roses onto the floor and fumbled to pick them up.

"If that's not a compliment, I don't know what is." Tony crooked his finger and beckoned Dayton to the bed.

Dayton set the flowers on the nightstand and kicked off his shoes. He jumped onto the bed and crawled on top of Tony, straddling his hips. Back and forth Dayton rubbed his ass over Tony's cock. Tony sighed and bit his bottom lip.

"I don't normally make house calls," Dayton said. He leaned forward and kissed Tony's neck before dragging his tongue over the olive-toned flesh to Tony's ear.

"Well, I guess I'm lucky then," Tony said, "because I'm afraid I'll die if I can't be inside you."

Dayton grabbed Tony's hand and shoved it inside his khakis. Tony squeezed Dayton's erection, eliciting a sigh from Dayton.

When the button on Dayton's khakis popped, he swore. "Damn it, I'm running out of pants for work. You've got to stop doing that."

"I'll buy you more. Just shut up and let me fuck you," Tony said. To stave off further complaints, he planted his mouth firmly against Dayton's and pushed his tongue into Dayton's mouth.

132

Dayton sat up and allowed Tony to pull his pants down over his ass, freeing his erection from the constricting fabric prison. He gasped when Tony grabbed his ass in both hands and pulled him forward. The gasp gave way to a moan when Tony's lips wrapped around the head of his cock and pulled several inches into his hungry mouth.

Dayton wrapped his fingers in Tony's hair and held his head in place. With short, fast strokes, he fucked Tony's mouth. He pressed deeper and deeper until he thrust well beyond the back of Tony's mouth. The constricting confines of Tony's throat drove Dayton to the brink, and he came without meaning to.

"Sorry…sorry," he panted. "You're so damn good at sucking dick. Can't," he moaned and sat back on Tony's crotch, "can't control myself when you do that."

Tony licked his lips. "I'm not complaining. Believe me." He moved Dayton to the side and stood up. "I'm going to get some lube. Get naked and be ready when I get back. Your ass is going to make up for your early orgasm."

While Tony went to find lube, Dayton stripped out of his clothes. An incessant chime filled the air, and Dayton looked at the phone sitting on the nightstand next to the box of roses. The screen displayed a text message preview: When are we meeting? Landing soon. Have missed you. S

Dayton picked up the phone and turned to face Tony when he re-entered the room. Tony's gaze went to the phone, and a confused look crawled across his face.

"What's up?" Tony asked.

"Who's S?" Dayton tossed the phone on the bed and sat down beside it.

"It's not what you think."

"The fact that you say that first tells me differently." Dayton grabbed his pants and started pulling them on. "I want you to leave."

"Dayton, please, honestly, it's nothing like that." Tony moved toward him and reached out for his shoulder. Dayton pulled away.

"Leave. I'm not going to tell you again." He leaned forward and pressed his face against his palms. "I'm such an idiot," he whispered to himself. "I'm such an idiot."

"You're not an idiot; you're just not listening. Please give me a chance to explain." Tony's voice didn't waver or lose any of its normal assuredness.

"There's nothing to explain." Dayton tried to button his pants and remembered Tony had made that impossible. He bunched the material in his fist and stalked out of the room to the front door. It bounced against the wall when he tore it open.

A few minutes later Tony walked out of the bedroom, fully dressed. He stepped out and turned around to face Dayton. The door slammed in his face and obscured his final attempt at an appeal.

† † †

"Ok, let me get this straight," Jimmy said. "All of this self-pity, drink yourself to death, puke all over your porch on a regular basis bullshit is because you broke up with a hot guy?"

"You're an ass. Tony wasn't just some guy I met for a one-time fuck. I loved him."

"Not enough to give him the benefit of the doubt. It was one text message. Did he ever give you any reason to disbelieve him?"

Dayton scowled. The anger crept upon him and settled into his guts faster than it should have, but he didn't try to stop it. Anger was better than hating himself for doing exactly what Jimmy had said. Dayton walked out onto his front porch, slammed the headphones over his ears, and fired up his receiving equipment.

After fifteen minutes, Jimmy gave up trying to apologize and went home. Dayton turned up the volume to where the sound of static became unbearable just to drown out the plaintive wailing of his brother. All he had to show for opening up to someone he thought he could trust was a massive headache and a heaping dose of shame and embarrassment.

Damn Jimmy for putting into words what he had been thinking all along. How easy it had been to just drink and blame everything on Tony. Now that veil of self-deceit was ripped to shreds and lay in tatters at Dayton's feet. Not for the first time he thought of gathering up everything and leaving for…well, he didn't know where. At least once he got to that elusive somewhere, no one would know his shame.

Except me, of course.

Suddenly, the static assaulting his ears broke, and he heard, "Vin to Z'Nor. Do you receive my transmission?"

Dayton glanced over his shoulder, searching for the source of the voice before he realized that it had come from his headphones. He looked at the dishes. They had stopped, pointing just to the southeast of the full moon that hung low in the evening sky. A quick glance confirmed his equipment was recording.

"Vin to Z'Nor. Please respond. This is an emergency. Do you copy?"

"I am receiving your transmission, Vin. Why have you broken radio silence before the appointed time?"

"My craft has been damaged by a micro-meteor shower on the dark side of the moon," the first voice said. "I will enter Earth's atmosphere in less than ten minutes. All flight and stabilization controls are damaged, and I cannot repair them in time. I attempted to engage an automated return course to Kallos, but it proved unsuccessful."

After a few seconds of silence, the response came. "I understand, Vin. I have modified the Earth equipment to scan for your signal. According to my calculations, you should come down in the middle of the North American continent. Engage survival protocols once you land—if you are able. I will retrieve you soon. End transmission."

In disbelief, Dayton played back the message to ensure he had not been dreaming. Still not convinced the transmission was not a hoax, he dragged a microphone from beside the computer monitor and said, "Vin, do you copy?"

Nothing. He attempted the plea again.

A sound like a thousand jet planes taking off at once shook the ground. Overhead a massive fireball streaked across the night sky; a concussive sonic boom rattled the mobile home. All of the windows exploded in a showering rain of jagged glass when a shockwave struck a few seconds later.

Dayton leapt from his porch and brushed stray fragments of glass from his hair. In the distance, the fireball disappeared behind a small group of hills, followed by an earth-shaking cacophony.

Without hesitation, he jumped into his pickup and sped off toward the crash site.

III

Tony put his car into park. He leaned over the steering wheel, looking first left and then right, attempting to see down each road that stretched before him. Snatching the map from the passenger's seat, he muttered to himself. The dusty back road was nowhere on the map. His phone couldn't find a GPS signal.

And the heat! It put him in mind of the ninth layer of hell. The air conditioner in the car stood no hope in the battle he had set before it. The humidity seemed to leech the cold from the interior.

He kicked open the door, stepped out, and slammed the door back, feeling somewhat better with the emotional outburst. Shading his eyes with his hand, he peered around, able to see for miles and miles. Just sagebrush, red earth, and telephone poles as far as he could see.

"Damn it, Dayton, why did you have to come here of all places?" he grumbled. His shirt stuck to his skin, which didn't help his mood. He peeled it off and wished he could do the same to his flesh just to get some relief from the sticky, tacky feeling covering his entire body. Rivulets of sweat streaked down his tanned, V-shaped upper body.

He consulted the map again. It offered as little help as it had before, but he had no better ideas. Then, from the west, a red mud-splattered pickup came into view, kicking up a small dust cloud in its wake. Tony waved his arms over his head in an attempt to flag down the driver, who saw him at the last second and fishtailed to a halt that stirred up more dust.

Tony wiped futilely at the dirt that now covered him from head to toe—and clung to his sweat-soaked skin like a suffocating blanket. The driver of the pickup rolled down his window.

"Howdy, stranger. You needin' help or somethin'?"

Tony laughed in spite of himself, giving up the futile effort of scrubbing the red dirt from his skin. "Oh, I need help, alright." He turned to see the man looking him over and licking his lips. Tony sauntered to the pickup, giving him all the show he could handle. "Do you happen to know where I can find a man by the name of Dayton Fitzgerald?"

The man—who Tony figured to be twenty something—pried his gaze from the muscular chest in front of him, locking onto Tony's emerald eyes. He shifted in his seat, to adjust for a growing erection, if Tony wasn't mistaken.

"Why you lookin' for D?"

"Pardon my lack of manners." He extended his hand and gave a firm handshake, holding it longer than necessary. "Dr. Tony Zellner."

"Billy. Billy Wilkes."

"It is such a pleasure to meet you, Billy." Tony smiled. He could tell Billy didn't want to release his hand. "Dr. Fitzgerald—that is, D—is a friend of mine. I've come to discuss something important with him."

"Is it that alien stuff D is always goin' on 'bout?" Billy asked. "Crazy stuff, if you ask me. But, if you know about that, you sure know D. He lives in a mobile home about seven miles that way." He pointed in the direction he faced. "Tell you what, you hop in your car, and I'll take you to him."

Tony smiled, "Deal. You have no idea how happy I am to have met you."

† † †

Billy stepped back from the front door. "Guess he ain't home right now." He pulled the door open and took a step inside.

"Hey! What are you doing? You can't just go in there," Tony protested.

"We do things differently 'round here, sir," Billy said. "Nobody locks their doors, and people have morals and respect for others' property. D won't mind that we go in. He trusts me."

It didn't feel right to Tony; he knew he was the last person Dayton wanted to see. Staring up at the sun, he decided that cool shelter trumped his misgivings. He stepped inside and pulled the door shut.

"This you?" Billy asked from farther in the room.

When his eyes adjusted to the darker living room of the mobile home, Tony saw the picture of him and Dayton together, their arms around one another.

"Yup, that's me," he said.

"Are you two—"

"Together?" There was no response except averted eyes. Tony forced a smile that held no joy. "Used to be."

Billy put the photo down, fidgeting. "What's it like?"

Tony stepped closer, pressing into Billy's personal bubble. "What?"

Unable to retreat because of the bar behind him, Billy let his eyes travel from the bulging crotch before him up the chest that he obviously longed to massage and then to fascinating green eyes. "You know…bein' with a, a man." He swallowed, hard.

Tony grabbed Billy's hands and placed them on his dust-covered pecs, which he flexed. "It's amazing," Tony sighed. "The best thing since sliced bread."

Both men jumped when the front door opened and slammed into the side of the mobile home. "Billy, who the hell—" The rest of the sentence lodged in Dayton's throat. His eyes opened wide when he saw Billy's hands resting on Tony's chest. Both men had obvious erections straining in their pants.

"What are you doing here?" Dayton tried to put more anger and less happy surprise into his voice.

"I brought him," Billy said. "He said he was a friend of yours. And the picture and all." The words erupted from his mouth. He snatched his hands away and stepped around Tony.

Dayton held up his hands. "It's okay, Billy. I'm not mad at you. Why don't you just go home? We'll talk later."

Nodding his head in mute acceptance, Billy cast a final look at Tony. "Nice to meet you. Hope to see you 'round."

"Thanks, Billy. Later." Tony winked at him and flexed his pecs again.

When the sound of Billy's pick-up disappeared into the distance, the two men stared at one another. Dayton's nostrils flared; thoughts flew through his mind at light speed. Tony jammed his hands in his pockets. His dick deflated, but he didn't appear the least bit embarrassed to have been caught.

"Well, I guess some things never change, do they?" Dayton asked.

"I told you I didn't cheat on you."

"I didn't say anything about cheating," Dayton said. He hated the defensive tone of his voice.

"Yeah, you kind of did." Tony held up his hands. "No, I don't want to do this. I don't want to fight. That's not why I'm here."

"Get out."

"I heard you. Last night."

"You heard the transmission too?" Dayton asked. He felt his pulse quicken, and he had to remind himself he was upset or else his glee would overwhelm his defenses.

"Yeah, I did." Tony smiled. "Pretty amazing, huh?"

"So SETI sent you out here to investigate? Wait, how did you know that the alien crashed here?" Dayton asked.

"Well, I didn't know for sure that it had. I knew it was somewhere in this general area. I've encountered other people looking for it, but they all think it's a meteor, not a space ship," Tony said. "Do you know where it is?"

"I thought I did, but when I went searching for it, I couldn't find it. Anywhere," he said. "It's like it never happened even though I know it did. Hell, that's why there are no windows here anymore."

"Shock wave?"

"You could say that," Dayton said. "That damn thing was so close overhead that I could almost touch it. I was sure I could find the crash site, but when I got to where I thought it should be it's as if nothing happened. No trench. No burning vegetation. No little green men. Nothing."

"Would you show me where you looked?"

Dayton stepped back. "Why? Are you just the precursor to someone claiming credit for my discovery?"

"No. No, I promise. Nobody at SETI even knows about this. I deleted the recordings of the transmission," Tony said.

"You...deleted proof of actual alien life?! Are you out of your mind?" Dayton shouted.

"Well, after I heard your voice, I figured that you would have recordings. Besides, after the way things ended..." His words trailed off, and he stared at the wall behind Dayton.

Dayton couldn't believe what he heard. Words refused to form into coherent sentences. He planted a long, hard kiss on Tony's lips. After a few seconds, he stepped back and turned away so Tony wouldn't see the redness that suffused his cheeks.

"Sorry," Dayton muttered.

"Don't be. I like it," Tony said.

"Well, don't get used to it." Dayton went to the fridge and downed a beer. He tossed the empty bottle into the trash. "I assume you brought clothes. You get a shower while I bring in your luggage. You can sleep on the couch."

"Will you show me where you think the ship crashed?" Tony asked.

"I'll have to think about it." Dayton walked onto the porch and turned, looking deep into the fire-emerald eyes that still beguiled him. "I don't know that I can trust you. I don't know if I even like you."

Closing the door, he walked to the car to start unloading luggage.

I don't even know why I'm letting him stay, he lied to himself.

IV

"Why is it so damned hot?" Tony yelled from the living room. He twisted on the couch, hating the fact that every part of him stuck to every part of the faux-leather torture chamber.

"Because it's Oklahoma, in summer, and turning on an air conditioner won't do any good without any damn windows," Dayton shouted back. "It's only going to get worse, so hope and pray the guy comes tomorrow to replace them."

"I'm right here. You can stop shouting."

Dayton sat up in his bed. Since all the sheets and blankets were on the floor, he had no way to cover his nakedness. He didn't want Tony to get ideas, but he was too hot to care.

"You're more than welcome to go get a motel room in town," Dayton said.

"One, don't think I haven't thought about it. Two, town is fifteen miles away via dirt roads that I couldn't even navigate in daylight. And three, I don't want to," Tony said.

"Why not?"

"Because I want to be here with you."

"You need to realize that we're finished," Dayton said.

Tony leaned against the door jamb of Dayton's bedroom. "You may not want to admit it out loud, but when you saw me putting the moves on Billy today, the look on your face betrayed you. You still have feelings for me."

Dayton jumped out of bed and stomped around to stand in front of Tony. In the confines of the trailer house bedroom it wasn't as imposing or dramatic as he would have like it to be, but it would have to do.

"It doesn't matter what my feelings are. This is all your damn fault. Stop trying to make me feel like I'm the one who fucked us up. I'm not!"

"I've tried telling you that I wasn't cheating," Tony said. He put his hand on Dayton's heaving chest, resting it barely against the slick skin.

"If it wasn't cheating, then what was it?" Dayton demanded.

"You wouldn't believe me."

"You didn't give me a chance to believe you," Dayton said.

"You didn't give me a chance to explain." Tony rubbed his hand in small circles on Dayton's chest until Dayton realized what was happening and back up.

"I'm listening now. Explain"

Tony took a deep breath, held it, and then blew it out slowly over several seconds. "I..." He took another breath. "I can't. I'm sorry."

"Get out."

"What?"

"Get out! Get the fuck out. Now!" Dayton shouted.

"Um, did you miss the part where I said I'd get lost trying to get to town?" Tony asked.

"I don't care. Get lost. Let coyotes eat you. Hell, let them fuck your dead body. I don't care. Just get out." Dayton pushed him backward.

"Look, I'm sorry." Tony took a step back and put his hands up in surrender. "Can we just calm down? I don't want to try to find the town in the dark. The map is shit, and I can't get a good signal on my phone for GPS out here."

"I. Don't. Care." Dayton pushed him backward again.

"What about the alien? We're supposed to work together to find it."

"Yet another thing you should have thought of." Dayton pushed him a final time. They had made it to the living room, where the door stood wide open to let in a non-existent breeze. "Don't come back."

Tony stepped backwards onto the porch. Dayton slammed the door and locked it with a satisfying click.

"I need clothes and my keys," Tony said, pounding on the door with the palm of his hand.

His phone, keys, and wallet flew from a glass-less window a few feet away, clattering onto the porch. He stalked over to retrieve them, muttering to himself. He could press the issue and get his clothes if he wanted, but that would lead to more fighting, and he didn't want that.

He sighed. That wasn't how things were supposed to go.

Tiptoeing to his car—cursing when the occasional sand burr dug into the bottoms of his tender feet—he started the engine and put the AC on full blast. Even though the leather stuck to his flesh, the welcome relief of the cool air made the sweat on his chest and forehead feel like it was freezing.

After cooling down, he thumbed on his phone, ignoring the small crack in the bottom part of the screen. Sure enough, no signal. He eyed the map lying on the floorboard of the passenger side and groaned.

"Damn it." He rested his forehead on the steering wheel. "I'm an alien. Just say it. I'm an alien, and my alien husband crashed nearby. I need help finding him. Just say it, damn it."

He thought about going up and attempting to apologize, attempting to drag the words "I'm an alien" out of the pit of his stomach. It was pointless, though. He knew when Dayton was in this state no amount of words would bring him back. Only time would do that, and he didn't want to wait. He needed somewhere cool to sleep and get his thoughts in order.

Town it is.

Within minutes he got lost. He had tried to pay attention when following Billy, but at night landmarks didn't look familiar enough to navigate by. His phone still betrayed him with no signal. The only hope was a solitary light in the distance that might be a house.

When he pulled to a stop in front of the old farm house, he remembered his nakedness. He doubted anyone in the middle of nowhere would open their door to a nude stranger at one in the morning.

A quick rummage through the interior came up empty. Thankfully, he could access the trunk of the car through the backseat so he wouldn't have to stand outside, naked. Within seconds he found an old pair of cutoff jean shorts. Shoes would have been great, too, but he could manage without.

The rickety wooden screen door made more noise than his knuckles did on it. When he heard something howling in the distance, he knocked several more times in rapid succession, but stopped short of shouting. A light came on, and the curtain hanging over the large window of the door moved aside.

"Hi, sir, I need some—Billy, is that you? It's Tony."

Billy opened the door, lowering the shotgun to his side. "Whatcha doin' here this time o' night?" he asked.

"Well, um, I got lost. Again. I didn't realize this was your place." Tony walked up to the top step. "Can I come in? I didn't wake your family, did I?"

Billy moved back, inviting him in. He smiled when he realized the young man sported a nice tent in the plaid boxers he wore. Looking down, he realized his own balls hung out of the ragged leg hole of the shorts. Now he remembered why he had these in the trunk.

"Um, my, um, family ain't home right now," Billy said. He put the shotgun on a shelf beside the back door and turned in an obvious attempt to hide his erection. "You're welcome to spend the night. I'll help you get back to D's place in the mornin'."

"Thank you, I really appreciate it." Tony put his hand on Billy's shoulder and squeezed it. "You're a real life saver. This makes twice you've come to my rescue. You deserve a reward."

Billy blushed. "No reward is necessary. Just doin' what anyone would do to be neighborly. Come in here, I'll show you to the couch."

Before Billy had taken two steps, Tony came up behind him. He pushed his crotch against Billy's ass and wrapped his hand around the cotton-covered cock that was already wet.

"I think you deserve a reward," Tony whispered into Billy's ear. He licked from the lobe up to the very top. "I've been aching to give out a reward for some time. Can't think of anyone I'd rather give it to. Especially since you seem to want it really badly."

Billy gulped and ground his ass in circles against the quickly hardening cock straining his boxers from the back. "I-I'm a virgin."

"I don't mind if you don't," Tony said. He kissed Billy's neck once, twice, and then dragged his tongue from the sunburn-darkened neck along the white collarbone. "You've wanted this for a while, haven't you?"

"Mmmmm."

"You want to know what it feels like to have a long, hard cock thrusting inside your tight virgin hole."

"God, yes." Billy licked his lips.

Tony wrapped one arm around Billy's chest while his free hand slid inside the back of Billy's briefs. He rubbed a finger along the cleft between the ass cheeks, pressing down until he found the quivering ring of muscle he intended to loosen up. Within the tight confines, he pushed against it.

"That feels amazing." Billy's breaths were short and gasping.

"Control yourself," Tony ordered. "I know it feels good, but I don't want you to come just yet."

"I'll do my best."

Tony pulled his hand free and spun Billy around. He had intended a slow, gentle kiss, but Billy gave in to desires that had been pent up and unrequited for some time.

Their lips smashed together like two storm fronts on the open prairie, and Billy forced his tongue into the gorgeous scientist's mouth. His hands were everywhere—moving over the rock-hard pecs, playing with the fur that covered most of Tony's body, cupping the low-hanging balls that were heavy with come.

"Let's go to my room," Billy offered.

"Here is good."

"No, I want you to fuck me in my bed. Please."

Tony smiled and winked. "How many fantasies are we fulfilling right now?"

"All of them," Billy said.

V

In his room, Billy turned and continued where he'd left off in the entry. His hands took in everything. When it became too much for his cock to bear, he stripped off his briefs and stood naked in front of the first man to ever see him that way.

Tony whistled.

"It's okay?" Billy asked. "Um, I mean, you aren't disappointed?"

Tony grabbed hold of the cock so hard he was surprised it hadn't fractured from stress. "Kid, the only way you could disappoint me is if you asked me to stop."

"I won't," Billy promised.

"But, if you do, I understand."

"I won't."

Billy wrapped his hand around Tony's hand on his cock and jerked himself with it. "Is it going to hurt when you fuck me?"

"Maybe. But don't worry about that," Tony said. "I'm a damn good scientist, but I'm an even better lover. I'll take care of you."

Billy whimpered when he felt the finger at his hole again.

"Lie down," Tony ordered. When Billy complied, he got down on his knees and kissed the virgin cock. "Remember, don't come. Not yet."

"When?"

"You'll know."

Tony leaned forward and swiped his tongue over the engorged head. He reached up and tweaked a nipple at the same time he slowly slid down the cock. His tongue and saliva bathed the rigid tube of flesh as he bobbed his head up and down.

Billy cursed and grabbed handfuls of Tony's thick hair, attempting to force the man to go farther. Tony didn't need any urging, and within seconds he buried his nose into the curly bush of brown hair.

"Oh my fucking God," Billy said through clenched teeth. "That's fucking amazing."

Tony swallowed, using his throat muscles to massage the cock. He wrapped his hand around the top of Billy's sac. Billy most likely had lots of practice jerking off, but there was a big difference between a lubed hand and a man's throat.

"I wanna suck you too," Billy said.

"Later. Just lie back, enjoy the ride, and leave everything to me." He went back to sucking.

Billy didn't offer any argument, only further encouragement in the form of fingers entwined in hair. With his mouth engaged, Tony used his hands to knead the firm globes of Billy's ass.

He drooled a little bit of spit and pre-come from his mouth onto a thumb and worked it in slow circles around the virgin hole he couldn't wait to be inside. Occasionally he would give a gentle push, but if Billy pressed against the digit, Tony pulled back to remind Billy who was in charge.

"Tony. Tony, you've gotta stop. I'm so close." Billy squirmed and tried to pull away. "Tony!"

The sound of Billy's wet member slapping against his stomach echoed from the walls. Wasting no time, Tony lifted the Billy's legs and dove tongue first into his ass.

"Oh my fucking god!" Billy bucked up, driving the tongue farther into his hole. His cursing intensified, as did his writhing, and Tony had to press him against the mattress with both hands.

"You're a wiry little shit, aren't ya?" Tony laughed. "I know it feels good, but calm down." He went back to work.

Billy moaned and thrashed his head around more than he did his body, but he couldn't lie still. Tony enjoyed the fact that his tongue drove Billy insane, opening him up for his first fuck.

"How...oh, god...How big are you?" Billy asked?

"You're getting ready to find out."

Tony moved forward, placed Billy's ankles on his shoulders, and pressed the head of his cock against the wet, sloppy hole. "The most important thing to remember is don't stop breathing."

"I don't know about this." Billy's voice wavered with obvious fear and doubt. "I want you so fucking bad, but I'm afraid. Sorry."

"We do what you want," Tony assured him. He rubbed his cock up and down Billy's cleft making sure he came nowhere near penetrating him. "Tell me what you want."

"Fuck me," Billy whispered. He closed his eyes and took a deep breath. "I want it, Tony."

"As you wish."

Tony pressed the head against the hole and leaned forward. Billy's back arched, giving Tony better positioning, and the head of his cock broke through the barrier.

"Sweet Jesus," Billy gasped. "Stop. Please."

"It's okay. Just take time to adjust. Breathe." Tony massaged Billy's stomach and kissed him, helping him focus on something other than the massive dick destroying his virginity. "How's it going?"

"Better." Billy's teeth clenched. His ass spasmed, working the head of Tony's cock. "Go slow."

Tony pressed forward. He had so much resistance to overcome. "You're so fucking tight." He continued forward, encouraging Billy to keep breathing. The constant pressure on his cock was almost painful.

Half full, Billy said, "You've got to stop. I can't take any more." He gulped in air. "I love your cock, but, god, I wish it wasn't so big."

Tony patted his stomach. "Let's see if we can make room for more." He backed out until just the head remained inside, and then he pressed back to the point Billy had said to stop. After a few similar strokes, he went just a little farther.

Billy's head went back. His soaked hair stained the pillow, and his moaned curses whispered from his lips. Without realizing it, he soon pushed against the cock and impaled himself with even more.

"How does it feel to have an entire dick inside you?"

"No shit?"

Tony winked at him and bumped his crotch against Billy's ass. "No shit." He held the position for some time, enjoying the feel of the tightness. He'd never experienced something so exhilarating. "Are you ready?"

"For?"

Tony pulled all the way out and thrust all the way back in. Billy's cursing started anew. Back in—flesh to flesh. Out, then in. Faster and faster. His balls drew up closer to his body. Not long now. He kissed Billy. He moved side to side, going at different angles, battering the walls that clenched and massaged him.

"Now," he said.

Billy needed no further urging. Screaming like a meteor crashing to earth, he fired salvo after salvo of come. It went everywhere. By the time he finished, he had covered his stomach, chest, face, and bed. One shot had even hit the wall.

Tony unleashed a torrent of come inside Billy, who licked his own come from his face. Tony leaned down, drew Billy upright, and kissed him. By the time Billy's breathing had returned to normal, Tony's cock had slipped from his ass, and he could feel a river of come following it. Billy kissed him tenderly and wrapped his legs around Tony's waist.

"You are so fucking amazing," he said.

Tony smiled. "You're pretty damn awesome yourself."

"Can we go again?" Billy asked.

"Oh, yeah." Tony pushed him back on the bed and towered over him. "It's time to learn how to use that pretty mouth of yours."

VI

Dayton removed his ball cap, and used the back of his arm to wipe sweat from his forehead. Not even noon, and already the sun baked everything around him. He stared down at the red Oklahoma clay dotted with sage brush and the occasional tumbleweed. A couple of turkey buzzards circled lazily overhead, looking for snacks or scraps of any poor creature that succumbed to the summer heat. Dayton took a swig from his water bottle, wishing the liquid was still cold.

He unfolded a topographical map and turned in a slow circle to get his bearings. If he calculated the descent trajectory of the alien craft correctly, it should have landed somewhere in the area he'd combed for several days. He just couldn't find it!

Dayton might have thought he was crazy or had imagined the crash if Tony hadn't confirmed the idea.

He shoved he map into the satchel hung over his shoulder. He ignored the added creases, a testament to his frustration and seething anger. He just needed to find the craft, make contact with an alien, become world renowned, and forget Tony Zellner ever existed.

A loud screech in the distance caught Dayton's attention. Shading his eyes from the unrelenting brightness of the sun, he watched one of the buzzards dip down closer to the ground. A few seconds later, the second bird followed. They both landed and hopped around.

They'd found something to pique their interest—most likely a dead rabbit or some other small creature. He went back to scanning the surrounding area. Nothing resembling a crashed alien ship stood out to him. He took another drink from the bottle, and cursed when just a small trickle filled his mouth. Time to go back.

By the time he walked the half mile to his truck, sweat soaked him from head to toe. Topping a small rise, he looked down on where he parked his truck. A dark shape on the ground in the small shadow cast by the Silverado caught his attention, but he couldn't identify it.

He made his way down the rise and walked somewhat out of his way so he could get a better view of what he'd seen. This far out in the country there was no telling what animal might have decided to cool itself off for a short spell. It could be a stray dog, or it could be something more deadly.

When he realized it was a man lying on the ground, Dayton sprinted to his side and rolled him over onto his back. The sun had done a number on the poor guy's face—several blisters had risen on his forehead and lips—and not one spot of exposed flesh remained white. Pulling his cellphone from his pocket, Dayton wished someone would bite the bullet and build a cell tower close by. Not that an ambulance could have gotten to him, anyway.

"Mister, can you hear me?" he asked. He didn't want to cause the man pain, but he needed to get him into the truck and to a hospital. From the looks of it, he wouldn't last much longer without help.

The man's eyelids fluttered open, and Dayton inhaled sharply. It was like looking into Tony's fire-emerald green eyes. The man blinked and groaned.

"Can you stand up?" Dayton asked. He brushed dirt and pieces of dead, brown grass from the man's thick auburn hair.

The man pushed himself up to sitting. He grasped the wet fabric of Dayton's shirt sleeves and held himself in place for a few seconds before bending one leg and standing up. Dayton steadied him as best he could and leaned him against the bed of the truck.

"What the hell are you doing out here?" Dayton asked.

"I got lost while hiking."

"Who the hell goes hiking in this neck o' the woods in blue jeans and cowboy boots?" He could have sworn the man looked afraid for the briefest of moments before bending over and throwing up.

"I need water," the man said.

"You need a doctor."

"No!" He turned so quickly that Dayton had to catch him before he fell.

"Mister, if you don't get to a doctor, you're going to die. Hell, you may die anyway," Dayton said. "How long have you been out here?"

"A few days." He looked up at the sun and then stared off into the barren distance to the west. "Look, just give me some water, and I'll be okay. I promise. I'm sure I look bad to you, but I'm very resilient."

"I'm fresh out of water." Dayton tossed his empty bottle into the bed of the truck. "But, I don't live too far from here. You can come and drink all you want."

"I appreciate it." The man stuck his hand out. "I'm Shepherd Kelvin."

"Don't think I've ever met anyone with that name before." Dayton walked Shepherd around the truck, opened the passenger door, and helped him inside.

Running to the other side, Dayton jumped in, started the truck, and turned the A/C to max. He set all of the vents to blow onto Shepherd before taking off. They bounced across the dusty, barren earth for a quarter of a mile before pulling onto a dirt road.

From the corner of his eye, Dayton saw Shepherd's head lolling on the headrest. The A/C didn't do much to cool down the cab, but he hoped it would help lower Shepherd's body temperature. He thought about going straight to the hospital, but since he had to pass his house anyway, he might as well get more water.

When the house trailer came into view, Shepherd leaned forward. The passenger-side tire hit a rut at the same time, and Shepherd's head connected with the windshield. He muttered a word that Dayton couldn't understand and rubbed at his head.

"Sorry," Dayton said. "Just what you need, a concussion on top of everything else."

Shepherd gave his head another vigorous rub. "I'm pretty resilient. You'll see; I'll bounce back in no time."

"I don't know of many people who can do that," Dayton said.

"I'm not most people."

"That's the kind of corny thing people in movies say," Dayton said. "Sorry, that came out wrong. It's not that I doubt you. I just don't want you dying on me when I could have done something about it."

"It's okay," Shepherd said. "I appreciate your concern and your help. I promise not to die."

"I'm going to hold you to that," Dayton said. "Oh, for fuck sake."

He slowed down and leaned over the steering wheel, squinting to help make out Tony's vehicle parked in front of his trailer. Dayton groaned and ran a hand through his still-wet hair.

"Fan-fucking-tastic," he muttered.

"Problem?" Shepherd asked. He looked from Dayton to the trailer and back again.

"Nothing I can't handle," Dayton said.

The truck came to a stop in its usual spot, kicking up a cloud of dirt that traveled a few feet before twisting and turning into a dust devil. Dayton killed the engine and looked down from his window to see if Tony was sitting in his car. A few seconds later his former lover walked around the side of the trailer.

"Oh my god," Shepherd said. He pushed the door open, stepped out onto semi-wobbly legs, and fell on the ground.

Tony ran toward Shepherd. Through the open passenger door, Dayton watched Tony scoop Shepherd up and kiss him.

"Of course," Dayton said. He jerked the keys from the ignition, kicked open his door, and stepped out. The universe hated him and wanted him to suffer. Tony and Shepherd ended their kiss after far too long for Dayton's comfort.

"Is there anyone you haven't—"

The accusation died on Dayton's lips when Tony began to glow a bright fluorescent green. Within seconds both men started to shimmer. They looked down at their dark-green exoskeletons and four arms, made brief eye contact with each other, and then turned to stare at Dayton.

"What the fuck?!" Dayton stumbled back and fell on his ass.

VII

"I don't know who the hell you are, but stay the fuck away from me." Dayton scrambled to his feet and turned to run back to the driver's side of the Silverado, but he wasn't fast enough.

By the time he made it to the front of the truck, looking back over his shoulder as he slammed his hip against the bumper, Tony's glow faded out. He stood up and flexed all four of his arms. Dayton could hear the hard chitin plates rubbing against each other. Tony leapt over the cab of the Silverado. He crossed both sets of arms in front of his body and stood waiting. Dayton stopped and watched him before stumbling a few steps backward toward his trailer.

Both Tony and Shepherd each grabbed him by an arm to keep him from falling over. Dayton struggled to get away, but he couldn't break free of them. No matter how much he kicked, thrashed, or cursed, they wouldn't release him.

"Dayton, please calm down." The voice held hints of Tony's voice, but the face was something else entirely. Tony's face was most certainly not human, but it didn't resemble an insect either—no mandibles or antennae. It looked more like helmet with green eyes, two nostril slits, and a wide gash for a mouth. "We're not going to hurt you. I promise."

"You're an alien, Tony." Dayton glared at him. "You're a fucking alien. Did you ever plan to tell me?"

"No. Yes. I tried. I wanted to. I swear."

"Mother fucker." Dayton took advantage of Tony dropping his guard to jerk his right arm free. He punched alien Tony in the face and immediately regretted it. He could feel the pain radiating up his hand from a broken finger, or two. It just added to his growing anger.

Tony gently grabbed Dayton's arm. "You're hurt. Let me take a look at it."

"You keep your fucking alien hands to yourself," Dayton shouted.

"Can we please go inside?" Shepherd asked. "Even with Tony healing me this heat is making me sick. I have no idea how anyone can live in this place." He released his hold on Dayton and took a step back. When he did, a shimmery haze surrounded him, and he became the auburn-haired man Dayton had rescued less than an hour earlier. Shepherd fell, landing on his knees with a grunt.

Without thinking, Dayton reached down and grabbed Shepherd's arm, steadying him. He looked up as Tony—human Tony—went to the other side and helped Shepherd stand. Dayton muttered a curse word before walking toward the trailer. At the steps, he moved ahead and opened the door, holding it so Shepherd and Tony could go through.

He looked at his truck, contemplated his chances of getting away before Tony could stop him, but decided to go inside. *I am a scientist, and this is what I've been waiting for.*

He closed the door behind him and went to get a bottle of water from the refrigerator. Back in the living room, he watched Tony running a loving hand along Shepherd's cheek. They both glowed again, just not as brightly as they had outside by the truck. When he realized he was being watched Tony reached up and took the bottle of water, helping Shepherd drink.

"How long have you two known each other?" Dayton asked.

"Since birth," Tony said. "Shepherd is my husband."

"You've been married since you were kids?" Dayton asked.

"Sort of," Tony said. "It doesn't work on Kallos like it does on Earth. We were paired before we were born, but the ultimate choice of mating was left to us."

"Are there female…"

"Kallosians," Tony offered. "And, yes, there are. Most of them are workers or queen mothers."

"So you are insects?" Dayton went back to the refrigerator for a beer. He leaned against the bar separating the living room from the kitchen and took a long drink. "I was fucked by an insect?"

"We evolved from insects," Tony said. From the gruff tone of his voice, the analogy had pissed him off. "But that would be like me saying I was fucked by a monkey."

"Touché." Dayton finished off the beer and put the bottle on the counter. "So, are you two advance scouts for an invasion force?"

"No, we're scientists," Tony said, chuckling. "We have no desire to conquer Earth. We're just here to study humans and the planet. We come in peace."

"Har-har." Dayton looked at Shepherd, who hadn't moved since Tony had given him water. "Is he going to be okay? There's no telling how long he was out there. Hey, speaking of which, why couldn't I find his ship?"

"Phase shifting," Tony said. He left Shepherd's side and stood in front of Dayton. He "We can't let anyone find out about us. I've wanted to tell you for so long, but I've been worried how you would react and what could possibly happen."

"I understand."

"I truly hope so." Tony put his hands on Dayton's neck and pulled him for a kiss.

Dayton leaned into Tony, opening his mouth up as Tony's tongue darted inside. He felt his dick harden and press against the denim of his jeans. Tony's arms made him feel warm, and safe, and...wanted.

"Um, your husband's right there."

Tony laughed. "Cultural differences, remember? Besides, part of my research is on the mating habits of humans."

"So I was an experiment, too?" Dayton said.

"You were one hell of an experiment!" Tony kissed him again. "Collecting data on you was an amazing experience that I'll never forget."

Dayton blushed. "So, will Shepherd be okay? Knowing what I do now, we can't take him to a doctor."

"He'll be fine," Tony said. "I've used some energy to heal him. Is it okay if we put him in your bed?"

"Sure."

Together they got Shepherd to his feet and walked him sideways down the narrow hallway leading from the front of the trailer to the back. In the bedroom, they gently lay him on the bed, and Tony kissed his cheek. Both of their images wavered, and Dayton found himself staring at the Kallosians in their true form.

"Stand up," Dayton said. "I want to look at you. The real you."

Tony moved to the foot of the bed and looked down at Dayton, who could tell the alien didn't know what to do with his four arms. Dayton ran his hand over the smooth green plates of chitin on Tony's arms, onto his chest, and then down to his groin.

"Where's, um…"

Tony took Dayton's hand and rubbed it up and down over the hard plate at his groin. Within seconds, the plate parted down the middle, and Tony's cock descended into Dayton's hand. Dayton got onto his knees to inspect it closer.

"It looks like it does when you're in human for, except it's, you know, green," he said.

"A genetic modification to allow me to fit in with your species and conduct sexual experiments."

"What would it look like normally?"

"I don't know," Tony said. "I've never been with any member of my species except Shepherd, and his looks like mine."

"Do you think he would mind if I…"

"Go ahead," Tony said. "Do you want me to shift back to human form?"

"No, I want to see what it's like to have you in your true form. I'm sure it's different getting fucked by someone with four arms and an armored body." He slowly dragged his tongue along the hardening cock.

Tony moaned and sat on the edge of the bed. One of his hands rested on the back of Dayton's neck, one slid down the back of Dayton's pants, and the other two caressed Shepherd's unconscious body. With alien cock gliding in and out of his mouth, Dayton watched Shepherd's groin plate separate down the middle, and Tony wrapped his fingers around his husband's dick.

Dayton undid the snaps on his jeans and pulled them down while taking as much of Tony into his mouth as he could. He expected Tony to be cold and unyielding in this form, but the warmth that flowed through his body and into Dayton was relaxing, almost intoxicating.

Tony's hand on Dayton's ass gripped, rubbed, and slid along the cleft. Dayton spread his legs, giving unfettered access. He reached back, entwining his fingers with Tony's, and guided a finger against his own hole. Tony's hand on his head pushed him forward to take more cock at the same moment he pressed inside Dayton.

Shepherd echoed Dayton's muffled moan, and his eyes opened. Propping himself on his elbows, he looked at his husband before making eye contact with Dayton.

"Is this an experiment?" Shepherd asked.

"I don't know," Tony said.

"No." Dayton stroked Tony's erection, twisting his hand over the head in the way he knew drove Tony insane. "This is me getting fucked by two aliens. If you want to collect data, you can. I just intend to collect biological samples."

He crawled onto the bed past Tony and tugged Shepherd's cock, which was identical to Tony's in every way. Tony pushed into Dalton, who felt warmth surge into his body.

The sudden sensation of having eight hands moving all over his body set his senses on overload. He had never experienced anything so...well, alien before. He could definitely get to a point where he loved this.

Tony pressed forward, and Dayton realized how much he had missed being fucked by him. So much gentleness and love just from the simple act of penetration.

"I love you," he said.

"I love you, too," Tony said. He couldn't smile in his true form, but Dayton could hear it in his voice.

Dayton felt the smooth chitin rubbing along his flesh. Moving his hips in small circles, he went back to Shepherd's cock, burying the entire length into his throat.

Shepherd grunted and then came in three rapid blasts. On the final shot, Dayton pulled back enough to savor the taste that reminded him of every time he had been with Tony. Simultaneously, Tony flooded his ass without even moving.

Tony, still firmly planted inside Dayton, pulled him up to a kneeling positon on the bed. "Taste him," he commanded Shepherd.

Dayton rocked up and down on the hard Kallosian cock in his ass and watched Shepherd move around in the bed. An almost primal instinct kicked in when the alien opened his mouth to suck his cock, and Dayton had to will the fear away. He soon forgot any trepidation, though, when Shepherd sucked on his cock. Within seconds, Dayton shouted and filled the alien's mouth with salty-sweet come.

Shepherd stood up, wrapping his arms around Tony and Dayton, and shared Dayton's essence with his husband. Dayton fell forward on the bed and groaned when Tony pulled out.

"D, Tony, are you guys—Oh my fuckin' god!" Billy screamed.

Dayton ran into the living room and grabbed Billy's hand before he could grasp the door knob.

"No, Billy." He wrapped his arms around the thrashing teenager and pulled him away from the door. "It's okay. It's okay, Billy, just calm down."

"What the fuck are those things, D? Let me go!" He struggled to break free.

"It's okay, Billy." Tony walked into the living room in his human form. He had his two hands held out to the side in an open gesture, and he smiled.

"Tony?" Billy looked toward the bedroom where he saw Shepherd in human form leaning against the door jamb. "What's goin' on? I just saw—what the fuck did I just see?"

"I'm an alien, Billy," Tony said. He stopped in front of Billy, come still dripping from his cock, and brushed his hand along Billy's cheek. "I'm an alien, and I'm not going to hurt you. I promise."

"An alien? But, but we had—Oh god! I had sex with an alien." Billy fell onto his knees and then sat down hard onto the floor. "I got fucked by an alien. Am I goin' to get pregnant?"

"No, you're not going to get pregnant." Tony laughed.

"No lizard baby or alien monster is goin' to burst out of my chest?"

"I'm not that kind of alien." Tony pulled Billy up to his feet and wrapped Billy in his arms. "It's okay. See, I'm not hurting you."

"Who's that?" Billy pointed at Shepherd, who ran his hands over Tony's back.

"That's my husband, Shepherd," Tony said.

"Hi," said Shepherd. "You're cute."

Billy blushed.

"Come on." Tony started walking Billy back toward the bedroom. Shepherd followed. "You want to join us?" he asked Dayton.

Dayton looked into the bedroom, watching for a few seconds while Billy and human Shepherd started getting to know each other.

"What the hell. It's for science, right?"

VIII

"I wish you didn't have to go." Dayton put his head on Tony's chest for a few seconds before kissing his very human lips.

"My shift is done," Tony said, "but once I've presented my findings to the Kallosian Scientific Hive, I can come back. Besides, Shepherd will be here while I'm gone." He pulled his husband into a hug.

"I know this is a weird time to ask, but where do your other two arms go in this form?" Dayton asked.

Tony laughed. "Spatial displacement and phase shifting, remember?"

"Right." Dayton smiled, kissed Tony again, and then backed away to give him time to say goodbye to Shepherd.

A pickup truck came bouncing over the rough terrain, and Dayton closed his eyes before the cloud of dust could blind him. When he thought it safe, he opened his eyes and watched Billy jump from the truck and run past.

"I made it. I'm sorry I'm late." Billy stopped in front of Tony, out of breath. When he could talk, he grabbed hold of Tony's hand. "Take me with you."

"What?" Dayton looked at him in disbelief. "You can't go, Billy. He can't go, Tony. Can he?"

Tony looked at Shepherd, who smiled and nodded once. "If you want to go with me, you can."

"I won't be dissected, will I?" Billy asked.

"Don't you think you should have thought about that before begging to go with an alien to another planet?" Dayton asked.

"No, you won't be dissected." Tony cast a stern look at Dayton. "As a matter of fact, you'll probably be adored and desired by everyone you meet. How would you feel about having sex with lots of aliens?"

"Could I, really?" Billy asked.

Shepherd and Tony laughed.

"We'll see," Tony said. "I don't know if I'm ready to share any of my human experiments yet." He hugged Billy, gave him a quick kiss, and then pointed him in the direction of the ship sitting partially visible behind Dayton's trailer.

After Tony and Shepherd said their goodbyes, Tony gave Dayton another kiss, hug, and a promise to return, and then he entered the ship. It disappeared, followed soon after by a sound of powerful engines pushing it off of the ground and into the sky. A plume of dust swallowed the ship, which caused a sonic boom seconds after it completely disappeared. Shepherd laid his head on Dayton's shoulder.

"Did he say when he's coming back?" Dayton asked.

"No. However, I have a feeling with Billy going with him, it'll be a while. That kid really is going to be the most popular thing on Kallos." Shepherd smiled and kissed Dayton's neck. "I know you're going to miss Tony, but I promise to try to keep your mind occupied."

"Well, my mind could go for some occupying right now," Dayton said. "How about giving me a little Kallosian TLC?"

About the Authors:

To learn more about the authors go to www.inkubuspublishingllc.com.

To learn more about Inkubus Publishing, check out
www.inkubuspublishingllc.com
www.facebook.com/inkubuspublishing
www.twitter.com/inkubuspublish
www.inkubuspublishing.submittable.com

Also from Inkubus Publishing:

The Bronze Dragon Chronicles, Vol. 1
Going for Bronze
By Gio Lassater

The Supornatural Collection, Vol. 1
Edited by Gio Lassater

Coming Soon:
Rhett Dane: Top Secret Bottom
The Adickted Trilogy
By Gio Lassater

Cover Design by:

TatteredWolf Studios is the joint venture of husband and wife team Brad and Megan Baker (otherwise known as Loni and Tatiyana Wolf). The goal of TWS is to bring their unique design aesthetic to the world through traditional, digital, and video game art.

They can be found at www.TatteredWolfStudios.com.

77184181R00109

Made in the USA
Columbia, SC
24 September 2017